"I wonder why you regard me with such disdain."

"I don't." Lyra forced her gaze down to the pages of the book, afraid of what he might see in her eyes. The air between them was thick again. Heated.

"Then what is it in your eyes that is so potent when you look at me?" Theron asked.

"Anger, maybe."

"Are you angry because I am here beside you, making you nervous?"

Theron seemed to have gotten closer to her without even moving. She could feel the heat of his body pressed intimately against hers. His aura was sparking with a multitude of colors, like fireworks. Could that be what she was feeling surrounding her, caressing her skin like a lover?

"You don't make me nervous."

"I make you something." He touched Lyra's cheek with the tips of his fingers, tracing on down to her lips. "I can feel it skimming the surface of your skin. It's hot, intense, powerful."

Books by Vivi Anna

Silhouette Nocturne

Blood Secrets #11
Dark Lies #26
Veiled Truth #50

VIVI ANNA

A vixen at heart, Vivi Anna likes to burn up the pages with her unique brand of fantasy fiction. Whether she sets her stories in the Amazon jungle, an apocalyptic future or the otherworld city of Necropolis, Vivi always writes fast-paced action-adventure with strong, independent women who can kick some butt, and dark, delicious heroes to kill for.

Once shot at while repossessing a car, Vivi decided that maybe her life needed a change. The first time she picked up a pen and put words to paper, she knew she had found her heart's desire. Within two paragraphs, she realized she could write about getting into all sorts of trouble without suffering any of the consequences.

When Vivi isn't writing, you can find her causing a ruckus in downtown bistros, at flea markets or in her own backyard.

VEILED TRUTH
VIVI ANNA

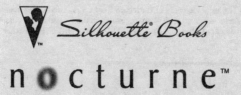

Silhouette Books

n o c t u r n e™

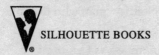

SILHOUETTE BOOKS

ISBN-13: 978-0-373-61797-5
ISBN-10:   0-373-61797-6

VEILED TRUTH

Dear Reader,

After so many wonderful e-mails about this series and questions about the next book, I'm thrilled to be able to finally share Lyra's story with you.

Lyra's one of my favorite characters—a strong, feisty woman who takes no guff from anyone. So I definitely had to pair her with a man who would test her every limit. Theron LeNoir is a man who doesn't take no for an answer.

I hope you enjoy her story as much as I enjoyed telling it.

Thanks again to my fantastic editor Tara Gavin, who had her hands full with this one. I appreciate everything you've (gently) pushed me to do. Lyra's story is much better for it.

A special thanks to my bestest buddy, Kimberly Kaye Terry, who is always there for me no matter what. Hey?

Happy reading!

All my best,

Vivi Anna

For my sweet angel, Shayla.

Chapter 1

When the uniformed butler opened the oak doors of the LeNoir estate in Nouveau-Monde, Lyra Magice tried not to be impressed. But she was—big-time. If the gated estate with the winding, stately, tree-lined driveway didn't astound, then the two-story stone castle would have.

The butler inclined his head. "*Bonsoir,* mademoiselle."

"*Bonsoir.*" Lyra loved speaking French; the sounds were so musical.

"Monsieur LeNoir would like you to wait for him in the parlor." He swept his arm toward an arched doorway to the right. "May I take your jacket?"

She shrugged out of her brown wool coat and handed it to the butler. He slung it over his arm and directed her to the parlor.

The moment she stepped over the threshold, Lyra felt like she was in a Sherlock Holmes book. The room boasted a huge fireplace with an ornate mantel over top. An old-style sofa and two chairs with end tables sat in front of the crackling flames. Exquisite artwork adorned the walls. Cherrywood floors were stylishly covered with oriental throw rugs. By the look of them, they were probably worth thousands of dollars apiece. Even the faint sweet smell of pipe tobacco laced the air.

She'd heard that Theron LeNoir was wealthy but truly she had no idea of the extent of it before now.

Lyra turned to ask the butler something, but he was already gone. Theron LeNoir stood in the doorway instead.

Looking the part of the wealthy homeowner, he wore dark wool trousers and a button-down shirt with gold cuff links flashing at the wrists. His dark hair was slicked back from his high forehead but unbound. The ends fell over his ears and brushed the collar of his shirt. At the seminar today he had tied it back, giving him a look of elegance and refinement. With his inky black hair flowing around him, he looked sexy and dangerous.

Smiling, he moved into the room toward her. "*Bonsoir,* Lyra. I am pleased you accepted my offer to come to my home."

"Well, I appreciate the invitation. It's not every day I get to see artifacts and books from witch history."

"Yes, I imagine a lot of things were lost in the immigration to America as well as during the persecution. Witches weren't the only things burned during that time."

Lyra tried not to watch him as he busied himself at the bar, uncorking a bottle of wine. He had a fluid way of moving, like a meandering stream of cool crisp water. He set out two wineglasses and poured the red liquid into them. Picking them up, he came to Lyra and handed her one. "From the LeNoir vineyard."

"Thank you."

He tapped her glass then took a sip, watching her over the rim.

Normally she didn't drink, but the polite thing to do would be to at least take a sip. Normally she wasn't polite, either, but his obvious pleasure at watching her drink prompted her to do so.

The wine was heavenly on her tongue as she held it in her mouth for a second then swallowed. It was better than she expected it to be.

He must've seen the surprise on her face, because he smiled. "It's the best wine in France. This particular bottle is over sixty years old."

"Oh, well, it's pretty good then."

Chuckling, he cupped her elbow and guided her toward the sofa. "Let's sit and talk. Catch up on the last five years."

Lyra sat but she really didn't want to engage in conversation with Theron. She'd never been good at that, especially with men. Attractive men, in particular. Or it could've just been her fear of speaking with Theron. Seeing him again, being this close to him, made her think about the time five years ago when she attended a spell-casting class and he had been there. He had made an impression on her then, and it seemed it was still lingering.

Her thighs were quivering something fierce as he sat next to her on the sofa. Not so close that their legs were touching, but near enough that his delicious cologne enticed her senses. A combination of spice and nature, he smelled like her herb garden in Necropolis.

"I enjoyed your talk today at the seminar. I didn't know you were an expert in demon summoning."

He chuckled. "I'm hardly an expert, Lyra. I have some cursory knowledge that was handed down to me by my maternal grandmother and a keen interest in the dark side of people. Witches in particular."

He stared at her while he spoke. His gaze was intense. Lethal even. She could hardly look away.

Nervous, she guzzled the wine down and set the glass on the side table. A drop escaped her mouth and it dribbled down her chin. Blushing, she was about to dab it, but Theron beat her to it.

With the pad of his thumb, he slowly wiped the red drop away. He held her gaze the whole time and she found she had lost her breath. He had the most amazing gray eyes. Stormy. Fierce. Dangerous. A caustic combination if she mixed in the fact that he was tall and gorgeous.

Definitely not the type of man Lyra usually found herself alone with. Men like Theron didn't notice women like her. She had learned that lesson years ago. Yet here he was looking at her as if he wanted to gobble her up in one bite. His sexual potency hadn't changed in the past five years.

Lyra sucked in a deep breath after he dropped his hand from her face and sat back, regarding her mouth with interest. His curiosity bothered her. There had to be an ulterior motive.

She had certainly felt something pass between them when they had first spied each other at the seminar. But that could've been nothing more than a magic recognition. They were both witches. Kin of a sort. Although he was a dhampir, born from a witch mother and vampire father, he possessed magic and some of the more loathsome vampiric traits, like an ingrained sense of self-importance. Or maybe she was just wishing there had been something flashing between them.

All she knew was that the way he was looking at her now made her nerves zing.

She jumped to her feet. "I'd love to see the books now, if you don't mind."

He leaned back against the sofa and studied her intently. Lyra had the sense he was laughing at her in some way. It might've been the way his lips twitched at the corners.

"I make you nervous, no?"

"No." Lyra lifted her chin. "I thought this invitation was to show me artifacts and tomes. Not to get reacquainted with each other."

"Can't we do both?" He leaned forward on the sofa, tilting his head to one side as if studying her. "I still find you fascinating, Lyra."

"Fascinating like a science experiment, I'll bet."

He stood and shook his head. "No, fascinating like an iris in bloom, or a caterpillar transforming into a butterfly."

Oh, he had to go and compare her to her favorite flower. She desperately wanted to swoon right about now. Inside a French castle, facing this sexy Frenchman would be a perfect opportunity to swoon. But the pragmatist in her swallowed the urge and took a step back from his penetrating gaze.

"However much I'd love to be a butterfly, I would prefer to see the artifacts you have. Unless your boast of amazing artifacts is only that—a boast."

He searched her face for what seemed like minutes

before bowing his head to her. "*Pardon*, Lyra. My manners have left me for a moment." He swept his arm toward a closed door on one side of the ornate hearth. "Of course, I will be happy to show you my collection."

Without waiting for her reply, Theron walked toward the door. By the way he moved, with his chin raised and his shoulders stiff, she knew she had upset him. Guilt squirmed around in her gut, but she pushed it down, refusing to allow it to soften her resolve. He was a lothario through and through. However much she might have enjoyed his seduction, she wasn't going to be a notch on his bedpost. Five years ago she had considered it, toyed with the idea of losing her virginity to him, but he had proved to her without a doubt that he was a cad. She'd never been a notch on anyone's bedpost and she wasn't going to start now with this man.

He could take his romantic designs, if that's what they truly were, and shove them up his perfectly formed butt.

"Lyra?" He startled her from her thoughts.

"Yes. Right." She marched to where he stood in the open doorway, an expectant look on his face.

The moment she crossed the threshold, her breath whooshed out of her lungs. His collection room was awe-inspiring. She'd never seen so many historical arti-facts and old leather-bound books in her life. She had thought her gran had an extensive collection of old tomes, but it paled in comparison to what Theron possessed on the four-tiered shelves that wrapped around the room.

She wandered across the room like a kid in a candy store. Eyes wide, tongue out, she nearly drooled at the sight of a large bronze cauldron displayed in a glass case in the corner. Chalices in silver, bronze and wood were arrayed on one wall, along with a bronze oil lamp in the form of a horned bird standing on one leg.

There was a witch's mirror from the 1400s, a wood-handled sickle adorned with black magical symbols, and a large display case of mandrake roots. She wanted to put her hand against the glass, hoping to soak up the history and magic.

"I can't believe you have all this." She circled the room, shaking her head. "I'm in complete awe."

"Come." He held out his hand. "I'll show you a few of my prize pieces."

Absently, she took his hand, too overwhelmed to think twice about it. He drew her to the far corner of the room and stood beside a lit glass case.

Lyra looked in and nearly passed out. "Oh, bless me. A maze stone."

"This is from 800 Ireland. It claims to be the map to Mother Earth's underworld."

"Goddess, it's beautiful." Lyra's fingers itched to trace the lines of the labyrinth carved into the stone.

Theron moved to the next item. "It took me five years to finally acquire this."

Lyra glanced into the case. A silver dagger lay on purple velvet. Ancient symbols were carved into the black handle. She'd seen a drawing of it in one of her witchcraft lesson books but never thought it was real. "Merlin's sword."

"*C'est magnifique, non?*"

"Yes, it's spectacular."

"And this?" He pointed to the next case, which was smaller but on a much higher pillar.

She looked in and lost her breath. "It's a medieval love ring."

"Yes, from the fifteenth century."

"Is there an inscription?"

He nodded. *"Mon coeur entier."*

"Which means?"

"My whole heart."

Lyra nearly sighed. The ring was spectacular. It was made of polished silver, and the metal had been twisted and shaped into an intricate braid. At the center was a love knot, making reference to the binding of two souls into one. To think some lucky woman five hundred years ago was given the ring by a man who loved and adored her. If only she could be that lucky someday.

"And now to what you've been waiting for."

Startled from her fanciful thoughts, she blushed as Theron led her to the middle of the room to another glass case. Inside was a thick, black, leather-bound book.

"This grimoire is said to be two thousand years old."

Lyra bit her lip to stop the squeal of delight she was about to emit. She loved ancient texts. She got her best spells from them.

"From the way you spoke about books the last time I saw you, I knew you'd appreciate it." Smiling, he nodded to the book. "Would you like to touch it?"

She glanced at him, unable to hide her surge of pleasure at the sight of the book and the fact that he remembered her love of texts. "Really?"

He pushed a red button on the side of the case, and the glass box slid to one side, opening it. Stepping out of the way, he gestured toward the book.

Rubbing her hands together, Lyra took a deep breath, reached out and opened the book. Instantly, the tips of her fingers began to tingle. The book was old and powerful. Residual magic still clung to it like spiderwebs. There was a faint red haze over the pages.

As she flipped the aged pages, she took in some of the spells. Some were of a common variety. Charms for love and prosperity. But others were written for more nefarious reasons. She skipped over the text, not wanting to invoke anything nasty by accident.

Her fingers halted on a page of symbols. She recognized some of them from the murders that had plagued Necropolis and San Antonio several months ago.

Three women had been murdered so far—their throats slit, blood drained from their bodies and ancient magical symbols painted onto their torsos in blood.

The crime-scene teams in both Necropolis and San Antonio believed they had solved the crimes, but Lyra hadn't been so sure.

"I know these symbols."

Theron glanced over her shoulder at the page. "Hmm, it appears to be an ancient demon summoning. Black magic that hasn't been used in two thousand years."

"This outlines what I've been seeing in a couple of cases still unsolved back home." She ran her finger over the text and symbols, excitement making her hands shake. "Could I take this book with me? I'd love to be able to go over it and translate these words. Maybe I can finally figure out what all the ceremonies really mean."

"Hmm, I don't think so."

Startled, she looked at him. "I'm sorry?"

He pushed the button on the case and the glass lid slid back over the book. "This book is much too valuable to be out of its sealed environment for long. I can't even imagine what hours of touching would do to the integrity of the pages."

"Didn't you hear me? I said the information in that book could help in more than one murder case."

"I heard what you said, Lyra. But you have no idea how much money I paid for that book. Maybe if you wanted to look through the book here, with gloves on, I could accommodate you."

"I have a plane to catch in four hours."

"Oh, well, that wouldn't be enough time now would it?"

She gritted her teeth. "No, it wouldn't."

He gave her that amused look again that nearly had her biting down on her lip to stop from screaming. "Hmm, I really want to help you, Lyra, but—"

"How about you pack the book up in an airtight wrapping and I can take it with me and send it back to you the same way."

He shook his head. "That won't do."

"Why not?" Frustration mixed with anger was starting to swirl in her stomach like a mini-tornado.

Ignoring her comment, he suggested, "How about I come with you to Necropolis and I'll bring the book?"

She flinched as if slapped. "No. Why on earth would you do that?" Her voice sounded shrill, panicked.

She'd spent years building walls around herself for protection from emotional pain, and she had a feeling Theron could be the one person who could and would want to break through them.

The last place she wanted Theron LeNoir was in her hometown. She couldn't escape him then, couldn't shut down the feelings that were beginning to surface.

"I don't know. It might be fun working on a case with you."

She shook her head adamantly. "Absolutely not."

"Why not?" He smiled, flirtatiously. It made her knees weak. She wanted to slap herself in the face for acting so foolishly around him. But he had that effect on her and by the way he was looking at her, he damn well knew it. "I think you and I would work well together."

"You don't have the right qualifications to work with me."

He lifted his eyebrow seductively. "Hmm. I don't know about that."

"Are you going to give me the book?" She sighed, trying not let her anger overwhelm her, but failing miserably.

"Not like this, no."

"Well, since you feel that way. I'm sorry I have to do this." Lyra flexed her fingers.

"Do what?"

Chapter 2

After a twelve-hour flight from France to America, Lyra marched down the hallway of the Necropolis crime lab. She knew she held the key to the murders that had struck fear throughout the city of Necropolis and the surrounding city of San Antonio. The book she carried weighed heavy, not only in her hands but in her mind.

"Lyra," Gwen, the lab technician, called, poking her head out from her DNA room. "How was Nouveau-Monde? Meet any cute French guys?"

She waved at Gwen but continued on. That was the last thing she wanted to talk about. She'd just about had her fill of those to last a lifetime.

She marched into the staff room where Caine, a vampire and her supervisor, and his human wife, Eve, who had transferred from the San Antonio crime labs, were having their supper break. She walked to the table and slammed down the huge book in her hands. Both Caine and Eve jumped.

"I think I found the real reason for the past four murders."

With his napkin, Caine wiped up the tea he had spilled from her explosive entrance. He crumpled the napkin, tossed it into the garbage pail then glanced at Lyra. "Good to see you back. How was the seminar?"

"Didn't you hear me? I said—"

"I heard you loud and clear, Lyra, but I still like to engage in mundane conversations once in a while with a colleague I haven't seen in a week. Helps keep my civility."

She sighed. "Fine. Have it your way." She sat in the unoccupied chair. "The weather was good. It only rained one day. The food rocked, and I think I may have gained five pounds. The seminar was enlightening, and I didn't snarl at anyone, even when they irritated me."

Caine smiled. "Okay. Now what about this big book you brought?"

"It's a rare ancient text that clearly defines the murders as ritual killings for the sole intent of eventually opening a portal to hell."

Both Caine and Eve looked at her as if she'd just grown horns. They should've known by now it was impossible, especially for a witch of her standing. Those types of things just didn't happen to witches. Vampires maybe, but never witches.

Eve ran her hand over the book. "Where did you get this? It looks really old and delicate."

Lyra closed the book and gathered it in her arms.

Eve shook her head. "You're as territorial as a lycan."

"I am not. It's just this book is, ah, fragile, and I don't want other people touching it."

"Did you buy it or something from an antiques shop?" Eve asked.

"Doesn't matter where I got the book. It's what I'm telling you that's important."

"We hear you, Lyra." Caine set his fork aside. "Go over the text, write a report about what you think is happening and we will go over all the evidence again to see how this fits in. Maybe it will open a new lead we didn't see before."

She nodded, satisfied. "Okay. Where's Jace?"

"He and Tala have a night off," Eve said. "I think they're celebrating a certain something." She lifted her eyebrows.

"You don't know that, my darling," Caine interjected. "Please don't start rumors."

Lyra looked between Eve and Caine. "What's going on?"

Eve leaned across the table, and whispered, "I think Tala is pregnant."

"But they just got married, for Goddess sake," Lyra said. Jace was the lycan on the team, and during the case they'd worked on in San Antonio he'd managed to fall in love with Tala, who had been a cop working for the humans. She'd masqueraded as one, as well. In truth, she'd turned out to be half human and half lycan and one hundred percent perfect for Jace.

"And I think they've spent most of that time in bed." Eve chuckled, but Lyra could see a flash of pain in her eyes. She knew Eve wanted children, and because Caine was a vampire it was unclear if they could conceive or not.

Caine set his hand on top of hers. "So did we, if I recall."

Lyra cringed. "Please. Keep it to yourselves." She really didn't want to hear about anybody's sex life, especially when hers was nonexistent. She was still feeling a little raw from the incident in Nouveau-Monde with a certain Frenchman. But she didn't want to think about it, and certainly not talk about it. No, she would keep that little secret to herself for as long as she could.

"How's Gwen doing on deciphering the DNA from the last case? Has she made any headway in determining what we are dealing with?"

During the last murder case in San Antonio, Jace, the lycan on the crime team, had battled with something, some alien creature that they still couldn't identify. The DNA they were able to collect contained both male and female chromosomes—an anomaly they'd never heard of outside of the amphibian kingdom. What they did know was the person, or thing, had definitely been involved in the murders plaguing both cities.

Caine shook his head. "Not yet. But we'll figure it out. With Jace's description and the skin samples we got from under his nails, we'll figure it out."

"Okay. I'll get started on the translation and get the report written for you."

"Lyra, you just got back. Why don't you take some time to go home, unpack and get some rest? You had a long flight."

"I don't think we have the time for that."

"The killer has been quiet for the past couple of months. I don't think a few hours will make any difference."

"And that's exactly why there is no time. Because he will strike again, and soon. I can feel it."

Lyra shivered, remembering her latest set of dreams.

Ever since she had touched down in Nouveau-Monde a week ago, she had started having dark, mysterious dreams about a man shrouded in the shadows. A man without a face who always seemed to be seeking…searching…for someone.

Caine covered her hand with his. "Are you all right? Is there something you want to tell me?"

She shook her head. No, she couldn't talk to Caine about it. He wouldn't understand. It wasn't the dark dreams that were bothering her, but the way they made her feel, the way the shadowy man made her feel. Her throat went dry just thinking about it and desire flicked at her insides.

Not a sensation she felt often. Actually, she could probably count on her fingers the number of times she had those types of feelings.

It disturbed her to no end.

Lyra squeezed the book tighter to her chest. "I'm fine. I'll be in the analysis room if you need me." She left before either of them could say a word.

Quickly and quietly, she rushed down the bleak hallway toward the analysis room. She didn't want to stop and chat with anyone. Too many emotions and thoughts twisted in her mind to have an ordinary conversation.

With a sigh of relief, she entered the room and set the book down on the table. Thankfully, no one else was using the room. Sitting, she began to thumb through the yellowing pages.

She liked her solitude, preferred it actually. Except she wasn't really truly ever alone. Her dead grandmother, Eleanore, kept her company. Well, her spirit anyway. Eleanore was a constant companion to Lyra, offering her wisdom and counsel when she needed it.

But since her departure from Nouveau-Monde, Lyra found her gran strangely silent.

Perhaps she disapproved of Lyra's methods of obtaining the book.

She was sort of happy her gran was absent and wasn't asking for an explanation of Lyra's actions. Maybe she could put aside the insistent pang of guilt she had in the pit of her stomach. At least for a while. Long enough so she could do her job. She usually didn't like to perform magic on someone, but Theron had asked for it. Or at least, she wanted to believe he had. He had offered to help her, although in his own way. Maybe she'd been too quick to act. The spell she'd used hadn't been harmful. Just solid enough to afford her enough time to take the book and get out before he could counteract. She'd used the binding spell once or twice before but it had usually been on fleeing criminals.

Shame at her action rose to the surface, but she stomped it down with a heady dose of self-righteousness. She was good at that.

As she settled on the right pages, Lyra took her pen and started to decipher the text and symbols. While her fingers traced the line and shape of the symbols on the weathered page, her thoughts returned to her trip to the Otherworlder European city. The rumors about the beautiful French metropolis were nothing compared to the reality of the place. Lyra had been instantly charmed.

But it was the guest lecturer Theron LeNoir who had surprised her the most. In more ways than she wanted to consider even now.

She could still picture his unusual gray eyes and the way they smoldered when he had looked at her.

To think, a man like that had actually smoldered in her presence. Lyra snickered, thinking about the oddity of the whole situation. She was definitely not the type of woman men burned over. A small low flame maybe, but not the full-on blaze she had sensed from Theron.

He was definitely a man accustomed to having beautiful, sensual women fawning over him. In fact, she knew him to be quite the ladies' man. During a magic seminar five years ago, she had considered succumbing to his flirtations but his fiery libido had scared her into rejecting his advances. He hadn't been hurt though, because the next evening she'd heard that he had slid into bed with one of the other attendees—a buxom blonde from Norway named Ingrid.

So she had been surprised when she saw him in the large conference room, standing at the podium. Their eyes had met and something had passed between them. Something—dare she say it?—magical. Lyra had felt the tingle all the way to her toes, and she knew Theron had experienced it, as well.

Too bad things had turned out the way they had.

Pulling her thoughts back to the important matter at hand, she continued to read and decipher the text. It wouldn't be long before the killer struck again. Four murders in the past year. Two times they thought they had found the killer, and two times there were proven wrong.

They were seeking someone who was not human or Otherworlder. Well, at least a *known* Otherworlder. They had DNA and skin samples that said the killer was much more than that. A species not known on any charts. Part vampire, part lycan, and part something utterly alien.

Eve had a brief encounter with the mystery figure

when she'd been kidnapped over a year ago. So brief she wasn't sure it even happened. And Jace had battled him in an alley, barely escaping with his life. Whatever he turned out to be, Lyra knew he was a ruthless, cold-hearted killer and they needed to stop him before he killed again.

Or all hell would break loose…literally.

Finishing one half of the text, she moved down to the second, more complicated half. The part she knew explained about the final ritual ceremony. She didn't possess the knowledge to decipher it. Theron did, though, yet he'd been too arrogant and so utterly sure of himself that she couldn't stand it. Those were traits Lyra despised in a man. It was most likely because of his vampiric genetics. It certainly couldn't be because of his witch background. Lyra had never met a dhamphir before. Half vamp, half witch, and completely foreign. But she couldn't deny her attraction to him.

Even now, her stomach flipped over at the thought of him.

She rubbed a hand over her belly and continued working. Her report wouldn't write itself. Well, not unless she invoked a dictation spell. Then she could just speak the words without having to write them.

Before she could consider it, Caine strode into the room. A look of frustration wrinkled his otherwise remarkable face.

"Is there something you forgot to tell me?" he asked, hovering over her.

She shook her head. "Not that I can recall."

"The baron just phoned." He leaned on the table with his hands, inching closer to her. Lyra had the urge to recoil. She didn't like it when Caine put on the power. It was like standing in front of a raging fire, with sparks coming at you full force.

"He's on his way to have a little chat with you."

"Really? Am I finally getting a raise and promotion?" she asked, trying to keep the nervousness out of her voice. By the way Caine lifted his brow, she knew she hadn't done a very good job of it. The chief had an uncanny ability to pick up on other people's moods. It came to him like a scent or taste.

She wondered what her guilt smelled like.

"It seems he's just received a call from Inspector Bellmonte of the Nouveau-Monde Police Department about an incident that occurred there."

Fidgeting in her chair, she avoided his gaze. "I can explain."

"I'd certainly love to hear it."

Lyra swiveled around toward the door. The baron, Laal Bask, stood in the doorway, his pinched face looking even thinner because of the way he was pursing his lips. He strode into the room. Another man followed in his wake.

Lyra could feel the blood draining from her face. Suddenly she felt very faint. "Oh, crap," she muttered.

Caine straightened and stared at the new arrivals. "Laal." He tipped his head toward the baron. "And you are?"

The other man lifted his chin. "I am Theron LeNoir, the owner of the book on the table."

"I see. Then I believe we owe you a debt of gratitude for loaning this to us. It will be invaluable to our investigation."

Theron's lips twitched, but not in humor. Lyra's

stomach sank into the floor. She buried her head in her hands and sighed. She was busted.

"Oh, you are mistaken, Monsieur Valorian. I did not loan it to anyone. Ms. Magice stole it from my home."

Chapter 3

When Theron entered the room and saw Lyra bent over his book, a look of fierce concentration on her face, his heart actually fluttered. The reaction surprised him. Most of his reactions to women were in lower places on his anatomy. But there was something about her that was unique. He had noticed it before, and he was certainly noticing it now.

It wasn't that she was gorgeous, because she wasn't. Certainly, she had some redeeming qualities—big, brown, soulful eyes; a wide, inviting mouth; a petite, nubile body—but it was something more. A quality that transcended physical beauty. Something almost ethereal in nature.

Standing now, her face stern and her hands on her hips, Lyra looked like a diminutive Amazon goddess.

Caine remained impassive, his brow cocked, regarding Theron as if he were nothing. Then he looked at the baron. "Are you taking this man's allegations seriously?"

"Are you calling me a liar, monsieur?" Theron replied.

"I'm sorry, but I find it hard to believe that Lyra, who has more integrity than most of us at the lab, would steal anything."

"Your investigator came into my home, bound me with a sophomoric binding spell at best, and took my book without permission. If that is not theft, then what is it?"

"It was not sophomoric," she grated out between clenched teeth.

Everyone looked over at her.

It made Theron chuckle to see the tick at the little witch's jaw. Magic surged out of her like a suddenly sparking electrical wire. He could feel it all around him. It surprised him how intense it was. She possessed power, this woman. More than he suspected she even realized.

"Lyra, is what this man is saying true?"

"No. Not really."

"Is it no, or not really?"

She shrugged. "It's complicated."

Laal huffed. "Well, someone had better start explaining because I'm very close to firing someone."

Hands clenched into fists, Lyra glared at the baron and took a step toward him like an advancing lioness. Theron swore he saw her eyes spark with flames. "You can't fire me because of this."

"I most certainly can."

Caine put his hand up to interpose. "No one is getting fired. I'm sure there is a logical explanation for all of this. Isn't there, Lyra?"

Hands still fisted, she halted her progression toward

the baron and turned her fiery gaze onto Theron. "If this stubborn jerk hadn't refused to help with the translation, I wouldn't have done anything so...so drastic."

His body started to sweat from her heated gaze. Oh, she was a firecracker indeed, this witch. If he had more time in Necropolis, he would certainly enjoy battling with her. He wondered if their battles would translate into something more passionate. Something they could take to a private venue, like his hotel room.

"I don't remember you thinking I was a jerk when you were flirting with me at the seminar."

"I wasn't flirting. You were the one hitting on me as I recall." She pointed her finger at him. "You were the one who invited me to your house, for a little midnight *rendezvous.*" She said the last few words in an exaggerated French accent.

Theron had the overwhelming urge to gather her in his arms and cover her mouth with his. To kiss the smirk right off her face. He could just imagine what all that spark and fire would be like in bed. It was too bad she wasn't really his type or he'd certainly try before he had to catch his private plane back to France.

"I was merely taking pity on you, *petite sorcière.* You are much too uptight and I thought you needed to...relax a little and enjoy what Nouveau-Monde had to offer."

The power she tossed at him nearly pushed him back a few steps. It was like basking in a forest fire. Her aura sparked and flared with orange, yellow and red. It was incredible to see. He ached desperately to reach out and touch her, to actually feel that kind of intensity on his fingertips.

"You son of a—"

"Okay." Caine stepped in between them. "Differences aside, are you looking to press charges against Lyra?"

"You'd like that, wouldn't you?" she growled, nearly pushing past Caine. "To see me in handcuffs."

Theron took a long, slow perusal of Lyra from toe to head, stopping at her pretty mouth. He wanted her to know full well what he was thinking. The flush in her face satisfied him greatly.

"My sexual peccadilloes aside, I would hate to see you in handcuffs, Lyra." He smiled. "I won't press charges, Monsieur Valorian. I think we've come to a mutual understanding and it needn't go any further."

"Well, now that the unpleasantness is over," Laal commented, moving next to Theron, "I can take you back to the airport where your plane is waiting for you."

Theron nodded to the baron, but frankly he didn't want to move. Standing here with Lyra glaring at him like a hungry tigress was exactly where he wanted to be. At least for a while. He hadn't had a reaction like this in a long time. Maybe never. Especially not to Lyra—a woman completely not his type. Prickly and combative, she shouldn't have done anything to his libido. But he couldn't remember the last time it had flared so hotly before. So intensely.

Had she been this intense the first time he'd met her? If she had, he couldn't recall. She had piqued his interest certainly. He had even flirted with her, considering bedding her if all went well, but she had skittered away from him in the end. The rejection of his advances had actually hammered his ego somewhat.

Squeezing the book tightly to his chest, Theron tipped his head to Caine. Then he cast his gaze onto Lyra. "It has been my utmost pleasure to see you again,

Lyra Magice. I hope we will meet again someday. Maybe we can get acquainted in other, more agreeable ways."

"Argh, you're so infuriating," she grunted, clenching her jaw so tight, he swore he could hear her teeth grinding.

Chuckling, he moved toward the door, following the baron.

"If I may suggest a way to resolve this."

Theron stopped in the doorway and glanced toward Caine. "I thought we already had."

"If what Lyra has told me is true, we really need the translation from your book, Mr. LeNoir. It would help us immensely in solving a string of murders."

His gaze moved from Caine to Lyra. She didn't meet his eyes. She was staring intensely at her boss as if she wanted to rip out his tongue.

"What do you suggest?"

"That you stay on in Necropolis for a few days and work with Lyra on translating the text and symbols."

"What?" Lyra sputtered. "You've got to be kidding. There is no way in hell I'm going to work with that man."

The vampire swiveled toward her, and arched one brow. "You said it yourself—we need that information, Lyra, to catch this guy."

"I could've been exaggerating."

"Were you?" he asked.

Defeated, she shook her head and glanced at Theron. He saw the anger in her eyes but also the desperation. Surprisingly, his heart had a little convulsion. It actually twitched with the way she was glaring at him.

He guessed he could stick around for a few days. Maybe he could squeeze in some extracurricular activities while he was here. Activities involving the witch and several uncompromising positions.

He turned toward the baron. "Would you please book me into your best hotel, Laal? Looks like I'm staying for a few days."

"Thank you, Mr. LeNoir." Caine tipped his head in gratitude.

"Please call me Theron." He set the book back down on the table and rubbed his hands together. "When do we get started?"

Lyra groaned and, glancing up to the ceiling, shook her head. "Why me? I was having a pretty good day so far."

Caine shook Theron's hand. "I can assure you working with Lyra will be interesting. But I can't promise you she'll behave."

Theron grinned. "Oh, that's perfectly fine with me. I always knew investigative work would be...invigorating."

"Oh, for Goddess sake." Lyra tossed up her hands and marched out of the room.

Theron watched her leave and chuckled to himself. Completely and utterly invigorating.

Lyra waited in the ladies' room until Theron had been escorted out, by the baron himself, to the hotel where he was going to stay. Peeking out the door, she watched as Caine came out of the analysis room then jumped in front of him, already in full argument.

"Why do we need him to stay on? Can't you just order him to give us the book?"

Without breaking stride, Caine shook his head. "Lyra, why are you arguing so vehemently about this?

We've had other consultants on cases before. You worked with that psychic well, if I remember correctly."

"But that was different."

Caine arched his elegant brow. "How?"

"She wasn't a pompous ass."

"You used to think I was a pompous ass."

"No, I didn't."

"Oh yes, you did. I remember distinctly the day you called me that in the lab in front of the whole team."

Lyra blushed. She actually did remember that day four years ago. But that was before she really got to know Caine.

"Besides, I just finished talking to this Inspector Bellmonte from Nouveau-Monde and he says Theron is quite gifted in magic and in other sensory detection. He could be a valuable resource for us on this case. Sometimes an outsider can see past the trees in the forest."

Lyra sniffed. "I hate that saying. What does it even mean?"

Caine stopped in front of his office and gave her that look she hated. The one that said she was being irrational. "It means you should go home, get some sleep and come back tomorrow, rested and relaxed and ready to work."

She opened her mouth to protest.

"Good night, Lyra. Have sweet dreams." Caine stepped into his office and shut the door behind him.

Huffing, Lyra stomped down the hallway toward the parking garage. She hated that she felt so uptight about Theron being there. The fact that she felt territorial about the lab wasn't lost on her. Six years ago, if someone had told her she'd be acting like a lycan with her pack, she would've laughed in their face.

Before she could reach the elevator, Kellen, the ballistics expert, slunk out of his room and leaned against the doorjamb, hooking his thumb into his front jeans pocket. He smiled that lazy grin of his as she approached.

"Hey, sugar," he drawled. "Missed you."

"No, you didn't. You probably didn't even know I was gone until now."

"Oh, I knew." He ran a finger just under his lips. "When are you and I going to hook up?"

"Like never."

"Why not? I'm a good-looking guy. I'm fun."

"I don't date vampires."

Leaning forward, he ran his tongue over his fangs. "You should try it. I give a helluva bite."

Before Lyra could respond, his pager beeped. He unhooked it from his belt, glanced at it, then set it back. Something in his demeanor changed and he nodded to her, no longer as carefree as he usually was. "Later, witchy woman." And just like that he slunk back into his room.

Shaking her head, Lyra continued onto the elevator. Leave it to the crazy vampire to relieve some of the tension she was harboring. He was so unabashedly male and flirtatious, nothing he said did she take seriously. At least for a moment, she had forgotten about Theron and the way he made her quiver inside in anger—and other ways she didn't want to name.

Maybe after a hot shower and some food, the sensation would disappear. She'd wash off the last twelve hours of exhaustion, catch a few hours of sleep, then she'd feel human again, or as close to human as she could get, considering her magic-laced genetics.

Once home, Lyra could barely keep her eyes open. The moment she slid into bed she had thoughts of Theron—his unusual gray eyes and full mouth. Pushing him from her mind, she reminded herself that he was an arrogant cad and was not worthy of her carnal thoughts. But as she slowly drifted to sleep, the last thing she envisioned was his elegant face and long, lean form. She wondered if he were getting ready for bed and what he was wearing. Did he sleep in the nude?

Then she dreamed. Of him.

She stood on a city street, in the middle of the road. It was dark; the only light glowed from two lampposts forming large yellow spotlights on the dark asphalt.

As she walked, she noticed the flow of the gauzy green dress she wore around her calves and ankles. It was soft against her skin. She wore no shoes, but the road was not rough or cold under her feet.

She continued to walk, knowing she was looking for someone. Someone who lurked in the shadows along the deserted street.

Fear did not fill her. Just the intense thump of anticipation sounded in her body. Sweat rolled down her back and her throat was dry. With every step, she knew he was coming to take her. He would soon have her, soft and pliant, in his arms.

She took another step but froze when she heard something rustling in the dark of the shadows. Had he finally arrived? She vibrated with eagerness. Would he be rough with her? Or gentle? She didn't care which, as long as he declared her his own.

Before she could react, a masculine hand wrapped around her arm and she was pulled into the black and slammed up against a brick wall. The impact rattled her a bit but she suffered no pain. Only desire, liquid hot, rippling over her body and pooling at her center. Then he was there, pressing his body against hers, his hot breath coming in ragged pants on her neck as he inhaled her scent.

Theron had finally come out of the shadows and claimed her.

She wanted to call out to rejoice, but she barely had time to take a breath before he was on her, nibbling on her neck and caressing her body with his strong hands. At first he was rough, biting at her neck, kneading her breasts, then the stroking became gentle. He alternated between the feelings, driving her mad. A bite, then a kiss. A pinch, then a caress. Pain. Pleasure. She became dizzy with the assault of contradictory sensations but she didn't want him to stop. Here she didn't possess any inhibitions.

Lowering his hands, he wrapped them around her buttocks and lifted her up, pinning her effectively with his body in between her legs. Holding her with one hand, he tore at the fabric of her dress to unveil her breasts. With no time to prepare, he latched onto her flesh with his mouth, teasing her with his tongue.

She couldn't breathe as he feasted on her breasts, scraping his teeth against her already inflamed nipples. Jolts of pleasure surged over her, urging gasps from her lips with every rough graze of his teeth. It was delicious torture as he suckled at her breasts. Laving his tongue over her taut peaks, he sucked in one nipple between his lips and rolled it repeatedly.

The sensation was too much. The pleasure too intense. Lyra pushed at his head, but it was to no avail. He continued to torment her flesh with his mouth. Unable to speak, she tried again to escape his fervent torture, but failed as he moved his other hand around her body to sink his fingers into her wet heat.

This time she did cry out, as he slid two fingers into her, stretching her, preparing her for more. She wasn't ready. He was going too fast. Bucking her hips, she tried to nudge him away, but the action only fueled his attempts and prompted him to go faster and deeper.

Panting and unable to separate one pain from another pleasure, she dug her hand into his hair and pulled. Yanking back, she twisted his face to hers. She needed to see his eyes and tell him to stop.

But when she jerked his head back, she lost all sense and screamed.

Half his face was gone, as if melted into the very shadows surrounding them.

Bolting straight up in bed, Lyra gasped. She had the sheets wrapped in her hands, twisted painfully around her fingers. Sweat covered her brow and upper lip, and soaked the back of her neck just under her hairline.

Gulping in breath, she slowly let go of the sheets and wiped at her face with the back of her hand. The dream had been so vivid. So much so, her heart thudded like a jackhammer and it wasn't from fear. Desire ran rampant in her body.

Once her breathing slowed, Lyra laid back into bed and turned onto her side, bringing her knees up. The ache between her legs would not subside. In her dream, she'd been able to fulfill her deepest desire—being with Theron. Allowing him to take her, she'd surrendered her desire to him. Giving him control of it. Something she'd never be able to do in the real world.

The thought frightened her to her core. Because even when Theron had been turning into something else, something born of shadows, she hadn't wanted him to stop.

Chapter 4

While sitting in one of the analysis rooms the next day, sweat trickled down Lyra's chest to pool in her navel. It even beaded on her top lip. Conscious of it, she wiped at her mouth with the back of her hand, trying to hide the evidence by transferring it to the legs of her pants.

The air in the analysis room was stifling. Or at least it was to her. It could've been that Theron was sitting much too close to her for her liking. Every time he shuffled in his chair, his knee brushed against hers, igniting a fresh brew of sparks that zinged up and down her body. Images from her dream last night kept popping into her mind. Theron nestled between her legs. Theron suckling at her breasts.

Theron shifted, his arm pressing against hers. Another jolt of something she didn't want to name shot up her arm over her shoulder and zeroed in on her breasts. In seconds, she was out of her chair.

"Everything okay?" he asked.

"Time for a break." Lyra paced around the room, conscious of Theron watching her. She stopped and put her hand on her hip, arching her brows in question. "What?"

"Is it so terrible to work with me?" He leaned back in his chair with a casual air she wished she could convey.

"Yes." She continued to pace.

With a smile, he shook his head. "You are not a very good liar."

I guess I don't have your talent for it. That was what she wanted to say. To sound cool and unaffected by him. But it wouldn't be true.

As if privy to her thoughts, his smile widened. Her foot faltered on her next step and she had to put a hand out on the table to keep from stumbling. Lyra had a sudden rush of guilt. Five-year-old guilt. Being with him again like this, casually as if they'd been working together for a long time, brought it all back to her.

There was just something about the dhampir that elicited certain personality traits in her. She always felt as if she were in a battle when she was near him. Her mind and body were in a constant state of war.

"Five years is a long time," she blurted out, unclear why she decided it was a good time to bring it up.

His brow quirked and he stared at her as if he hadn't the foggiest idea what she was talking about. "It can be."

"Don't look at me as if you don't know what I'm talking about."

His lips twitched but he tried to hide it by ducking his head. "Lyra, are you saying that you regret rejecting me all those years ago?"

"What?" She gaped at him. "No!"

Eyes wide, he stared at her.

"Er, I mean, of course not." Her lips felt like balloons and she kept fumbling with them. "What I mean to say is the decision I made was a good one, at the time."

"At the time?" He leaned on the table, his beautiful eyes searching her face. "You mean, you wouldn't make that decision now?"

"Theron, don't complicate things."

"*Chèrie*—" he reached across the table and grasped her hand "—I believe they already are. You are much too dynamic and have this energy about you that I do not understand. It... You still fascinate me."

"Is that just your fancy way of saying I'm a bitch?"

Theron broke into a fit of laughter. His whole body shook from the effort. It was the first honest emotion she'd seen from him.

In turn, Lyra's lips twitched, then laughter bubbled out of her. The tension building between them dissipated into thin air. "It feels good to laugh. There hasn't been much around here to find amusing."

Sobering, Theron set his hands flat on the table. "I suppose not, with all the murders." He rubbed a hand over the page of the book they had been previously deciphering. "And you believe the answers are in here?"

She met his gaze and nodded.

"Your killer then must be very familiar with the black arts. There are only six of these books in the world."

"Or he has a black witch working for him," she offered as she came back around the table and sat down.

"That is possible, too."

She watched him as he bent down and started to read the text. From the moment she knew he had the book, she wanted to ask him why he possessed a tome that contained dark magic. Her skin crawled every time she touched the pages and read the spells. How could a person keep something like that in his home?

She hated black magic. It went against everything she believed in and everything she'd been taught, by those she loved, about upholding nature's balance. To practice the black was to skirt the edges of immorality.

"Why do you have this book?"

He didn't look up right away, but continued to trace his finger along the page of the book. Sighing, he glanced at her. There was something in his eyes she couldn't quite read. Something akin to remorse.

"It is an artifact from ancient times. It's worth quite a bit of money. I have many relics from different cultures in my collection. I see this one as no different."

"So it's a possession and nothing more? You have no emotional attachment to it?"

He leaned back in his chair, eyeing her suspiciously. "Why do you ask?"

"I'm just wondering what would possess a witch to keep something like this around. I know I could never have it in my home. It would constantly give me the creeps, knowing the potential for evil inside."

"It is not the thing that has dark power, Lyra, but the person wielding it."

"I suppose."

He looked at her for a long moment, as if taking in everything about her face. She wondered what he saw when he looked at her so intensely. Could he see the nerves racing through her? Could he sense that his presence was doing all kinds of delicious things to her body?

His intense scrutiny made her shiver. "What?" she asked in exasperation.

"I wonder why you regard me with such disdain."

"I don't." She forced her gaze down to the pages of the book, afraid of what he might see in her eyes. The air between them was growing thick again. Heated.

"Then what is it in your eyes that is so potent when you look at me?"

"Anger maybe."

"You are still mad at me for not giving you the book?"

"Maybe."

"Or is it that you are angry because I am here beside you, making you very nervous?"

He seemed to have gotten closer to her without even moving. She could feel the heat of his body pressed intimately against hers. His aura was sparking with a multitude of colors like fireworks. Could that be what she was feeling surrounding her, caressing her skin like a lover?

He possessed a lot of magical power. She could hear it humming like an electric razor building around him. Maybe his vampire side increased the flow of it. He frightened her on so many levels that she couldn't even contemplate them separately.

"You don't make me nervous."

"I make you something." He touched her cheek with the tips of his fingers, tracing one down to her lips. "I can feel it skimming the surface of your skin. It's hot, intense, powerful."

Gazing into his eyes, she should've pulled away. It would've been the smart thing to do in a situation like this. But she didn't want to. Not this time. She liked the touch of his hand on her face, his magic prickled across her skin. And she wondered how it would feel in other places on her body—areas that had no business quivering in response to this man.

Theron represented things she didn't like in a man and in a witch—arrogance, self-importance and an insufferable attitude. But still, from the very moment she'd seen him again, she'd felt drawn to him, as if he had some big part to play in her life. Maybe, under all his upper-crust snobbery and conceit, he possessed a redeeming heart and spirit.

He leaned toward her mouth, his gaze glued to hers. Her lips tingled in anticipation of his kiss. Her whole body thrummed like plucked guitar strings waiting for the press of his lips. She knew it wouldn't be gentle. He had too much passion for something as simple as that.

The pentagram at her neck stared to vibrate and warm. Instinctively, she reached up for it and pressed her fingertips to it. Something was wrong.

She pulled away just as Caine marched into the room, a look of unease on his face.

"Merde." Sighing, Theron let his hand drop and he sat back in his chair.

"What's wrong, Chief?" Lyra asked.

"There's been another murder."

"I knew it was coming. I just knew it." She rubbed her thumb over her amulet for comfort.

Caine's eyes narrowed and he leaned over the table. "Did you see it in a vision?"

"Not really. I just…felt it." Lyra could feel Caine probing her with his extrasensory perception. "Why? What are you looking for? What does it have to do with me?"

Drawing back, he rubbed a hand over his face. "You'll see when we get there."

"I'll get my kit." Lyra stood, as did Theron.

"Is there something I can do?"

"I don't know. Is there?" Caine responded.

"I can sense things." Theron licked his lips. Lyra could see anxiety rushing through him. "When I touch a body, I can get a sense of where that person was hours before."

"Could you sense that with me?" Lyra asked, concerned he could have some extra power over her. She didn't want him to know that hours before she came to the analysis room she'd been in the washroom splashing cold water on her face and mumbling to herself about him.

"Only the dead." He drew a hand through his hair. "I helped in a murder case about four years ago. You can call Inspector Bellmonte to confirm that."

Caine stared at him for a few seconds. Lyra knew he was trying to read Theron's emotions. And by the calm look on Theron's face, he had opened himself up for it, likely expecting it from the chief.

"Okay," Caine finally said. "Stick close to Lyra."

Lyra followed Caine out; Theron matched her stride for stride down the hallway. She glanced at him as they walked and saw a hard and stoic look on his face. His skin had grown pale. She could just imagine what he must be thinking.

To know the dead was one gift she knew she'd never want. Knowing the living was enough.

Black storm clouds rolled through the sky like a dark, unraveling carpet. Lyra thought it convenient that the sky's emotions mimicked her own. Shivers radiated down her spine. Even the warmth from the SUV's heater couldn't chase them away as they pulled up to the crime scene.

Both ends of the street had been cordoned off with

yellow police tape. But that didn't stop several morbid crime tourists from craning their necks to get a glimpse of the body. She envied them their distance because she was going to have to get close enough for the smell to permanently tattoo itself on the inside of her nasal cavity.

One would think she'd be used to the smell by now after six years. But death was an odor no one should have to get used to.

After she jumped out of the vehicle and grabbed her kit from the back, she glanced at Theron and wondered why he had offered to help. It was obvious by the stony look on his face that he wasn't pleased about being here. He actually looked afraid.

"Everyone ready?" Caine asked.

Lyra grabbed Caine's arm before he could walk away. "You're keeping something from me. I can see it in your face when you look at me."

"I'm not trying to be cryptic, but I don't want to taint your perception." He set his hand over hers. "Just prepare yourself. You'll get your answers when we get to the body."

Lyra let her hand fall and, kit in hand, followed Caine and Eve to the crime scene. Theron walked beside her, his eyes forward, a tick at his jaw. She had a sudden urge to smooth it away.

When they reached the police tape, an officer lifted it for them and they went under. There were two people, a uniform she didn't know and Captain Garner in faded jeans and a leather jacket, standing by the plastic-covered body in the middle of the road.

Mahina shook Caine's hand. "Nice day, eh, Valorian?"

"I'll save my verdict for later." Caine glanced up into the grumbling sky. "Let's hope that doesn't unleash on us quite yet." He gestured behind him to Theron. "Captain Mahina Garner, this is Theron LeNoir. He'll be helping us with the body."

The lycan nodded briskly to Theron then turned to look at Lyra. "It's good to see you, Magice."

"You, too, Captain." The police captain's warm greeting threw Lyra off. Mahina was not one to offer compliments or polite greetings freely. Something was definitely wrong. She started to fidget with her necklace, taking solace in its familiar smooth surface.

"Okay, everyone, take a deep breath." Mahina crouched down next to the body, gripped the side of the plastic tarp and lifted it.

Eve gasped. "Oh, dear God."

Nothing could've prepared Lyra for what she saw lying on the concrete in front of her. She now knew why Caine hadn't said anything. How could a person be prepared for something like this?

Her whole body shook as she stared down at *her* face on a dead woman.

Waxy, blue-tinged skin and stiff from rigor, it was if she were looking down at herself in another time. It was as if she were staring down at a deathly mirror.

Chapter 5

Lyra had to fight to stay upright. In fact, she had to fight to stay in that spot. What she really wanted to do was turn and run.

Theron set his hand on her shoulder, but said nothing. What could he say? There was nothing that could make this better, nothing that would still the way her body shook and the way her skin crawled.

"I thought it was you," Mahina said, looking at Lyra. "When I arrived at the scene and saw the victim, I called Caine right away to make sure you were still alive and kicking."

Caine looked from the body to Lyra. "The resemblance is uncanny."

And it was. So much that it made her stomach clench and her throat run dry.

The victim had the same face, bone structure, hair

color and hairstyle. If her eyes had been open, Lyra knew they'd be the same tawny brown.

"Is it a coincidence?" Eve asked.

Mahina shook her head. "Not likely. The victim's hair has been hacked off recently. I'd say to match Lyra's."

"I don't believe in coincidences." Caine continued to stare at Lyra. "This is a warning."

Finally, Lyra reacted. Snapping out of her shock, she glared at Caine, anger surging through her veins. It was better than allowing the shock and fear to paralyze her into inaction. Anger she knew. It was an emotion she had wrapped herself in long ago, as a way to deal with life's unfairness. "You're not taking me off this case."

"This killer isn't messing around, Lyra. He knows who we are."

"We're no more at risk than we usually are on a case."

"Jace nearly died when he was attacked in San Antonio. I won't have the same thing happen to you."

"I can take care of myself. My magic is strong."

"His is stronger."

Lyra swiveled around and glared at Theron. He hadn't met her gaze but still stared down at the body. His face was paler than normal, drawn in, haunted.

"Black magic is strong, Lyra. Binding spells and simple charms are no match for its power."

Her fingers twitched, eager to invoke a spell to purge her emotions. "I have more than simple charms in my arsenal, dhampir. So I'd watch what you say if you don't want to end up as something slimy."

Caine took a step forward, his hand up as if to ward off an attack. The action was futile. If Lyra wanted to cast a spell, there'd be nothing to stop her. "If you weren't alone all the time…"

That had her eyes sparking. "You want to take me off the damn case because I'm single?" she hissed.

"That's not what I'm saying."

"Then what are you saying, Chief? Because I really want to know."

"Let me assign someone—" his gaze brushed fleetingly over Theron "—for your protection."

"I don't need a bodyguard."

"A police presence then, when you're not at the lab."

She glanced at Theron, at the body, then back to Caine. "Fine. But no one is coming in my house. They can stay out in the car."

"Agreed." Snapping on latex gloves, he gestured toward the scene. "Now, let's do this before the sky opens up."

"Too late." Mahina had her palm turned toward the sky.

The first fat drops of rain splattered Lyra on the nose and cheek. A slice of white lightning dissected the black clouds, confirming Mahina's statement. The boom of thunder followed in its wake. The rumbling sound prompted the crew to action.

Caine, Eve and Mahina scrambled to get more tarps over the body and the area. Lyra raised her hands, palms out, toward the crime scene. She knew a protection spell that would save the integrity of the scene. Mumbling words under her breath, the beginnings of a yellow glow started at her fingers, but the spell wasn't strong enough. The rain was coming too fast.

Theron noticed the glow on Lyra's hands, but he could tell instantly that the spell wouldn't be strong or quick enough to protect the area. He moved in behind her, pressing intimately against her back, and placed his hands on top of hers.

Instantaneously, their magic mingled together into a ball of heated light. He could feel it prickle across his hands and up his arms. It was both exhilarating and frightening to experience.

She flinched from his intrusion but didn't stop mumbling the words of the spell. He could feel her unease with him so near but knew their mixed power would incant the spell faster. Gritting his teeth, Theron forced his magic from his hands and into Lyra's.

Years before, he had attempted to mix his magic with another's. It had had disastrous effects. Effects he still had nightmares about. That was when he'd been dabbling in black magic. Undisciplined and naive, he'd attempted to do a spell that would give him great power—power to rival his father's. But it had gone all wrong and his young, eager apprentice had been hurt. Shaking his head, he pushed the memory from his mind. He couldn't think about it now.

But this magic felt different. He didn't experience the same cold dread but rather a feeling of euphoria. He became light-headed and his stomach flipped over but not in fear or revulsion. He almost felt giddy with it.

Finally, after a few more seconds, there was an audible popping sound and a protection bubble formed over the body and crime scene in a ten-foot radius. The rain splattered against it and ran down its invisible domed sides.

Dropping his hands, Theron moved away from Lyra. His skin still tingled and he rubbed his hands against the sleeves of his jacket. He was uncertain how he felt about her magic still lingering on him. It wasn't unpleasant, and that was part of the problem.

"Good work, you two." Mahina gave them the thumbs-up and went about marking a search grid around the body.

Lyra glanced over her shoulder. "Thanks." He noticed that she, too, was rubbing her hands against the legs of her pants. His magic was obviously still sticking. By the look on her face, she was unnerved about it, as well.

"You're welcome."

He watched her as she moved away from him and started her work. Efficiently, she stepped through the crime scene, taking pictures and collecting evidence. He admired her ability to do this every day. It was obvious she had the tenacity and the desire for the job. He didn't think he could do it. Well, he knew he couldn't. After working a few cases with Inspector Bellmonte, hadn't Theron told him not to call again? That he was done helping the police?

So why had he volunteered this time? Watching Lyra gave him his answer. It was because of her. In some way he wanted to impress her, despite her prickly demeanor toward him.

"Theron," Caine called. The vampire gestured him over to the body. "I'm done here. It's your turn."

Cautiously, Theron knelt down on the other side of the body. It was difficult to look at her and not see Lyra lying there, cold and unmoving. Dead and decaying. He had to swallow the bile rising in his throat. It wouldn't do anyone any good, if all of sudden he lost his breakfast all over the crime scene.

With the victim uncovered, he could see what had been done to her. Symbols had been painted on her torso in red. Blood, he assumed. He recognized some of them from his book.

Now he could truly understand why Lyra had been so adamant about using his tome. Why she had resorted to stealing it from him in the first place.

"Are you ready?"

Lifting his gaze from the victim's body, Theron nodded. He wasn't ready, not by a long shot. How could anyone be ready for what he had said he would do?

Caine handed him a latex glove.

"I have to touch her skin. It doesn't work through any type of barrier."

"I'll have to fingerprint you later for the file." Caine shoved the glove back into his coat pocket.

"That's fine." Taking a deep breath, Theron spread his fingers out and placed them one by one along the girl's cheekbone.

She was like waxy ice. The urge to pull his hand away itched at his skin. The feel of her flesh made his stomach roil. To stop from retching, he had to open his mouth to breathe.

Pressing hard, he searched for the residual thread of memory that usually hung around after death. Spiritual energy was the last thing to leave after death. Sometimes it could even hang around for days or weeks. And in some rare instances forever.

"Getting anything?" Caine asked.

"Nothing yet, but—"

His hand grew colder and his breath came out in puffs of steam. A rush of images peppered his mind like a barrage of bullets from a machine gun.

Silver frost. White plastic. Streaks of red.

"A freezer. She's in a freezer like a piece of meat."

"The coroner suspected as much," Caine responded. "What else?"

More images came to him but they were running backward like film frames spliced in reverse.

"Gray cement. An oil stain."

"Like in a garage?" Caine prompted.

Theron nodded. "I see a tire on a vehicle."

"Can you see a make? Can you see a vehicle?"

"I see a three-pointed silver star in the center. There's a reflection in the hubcap. A car in a dark color. Black or dark blue."

Again the images changed. Theron felt like he was being yanked backward through a doorway. Mentally he tried to hang on to the last memory but it disappeared, quickly replaced by something else.

Outside in the trees. Night. The moon was almost full. Theron could smell wet grass and trees.

"There's a bunch of trees. A clearing."

His heart started to race and despite the cool misty air, sweat trickled down his back. He felt like he'd been running in the night. His lungs burned from the exertion.

"I think she was running through the trees. Being chased."

The trees melted away like a Polaroid set on fire. Tall concrete buildings replaced the picture. Garbled loud music thumped in his ears. He couldn't make out any of the words in the rapidly spoken lyrics.

"Do you see anything else, Theron?" Lyra asked. Her subtle floral scent came to him on a breath of cool air. It calmed him and he took in another mouthful.

"Buildings. Skyscrapers. A billboard. I hear music."

Then everything went black.

Moving his fingers, Theron tried to find any other remaining memory. But it was pointless; the energy had disappeared. It was gone and there was nothing left for him to see.

Rocking back on his haunches, he took in a deep breath and flexed his fingers. They had cramped during the process. "I can't see anything else."

Nodding, Caine flipped the plastic back over the girl and stood. "We're looking for a dark-colored Mercedes. And we'll start canvassing the club areas downtown. At least it's something to go on."

His body trembling, Theron found it difficult to stand. He felt like he'd been worked over once or twice by a mean-spirited thug. Wiping his hand on his pants, he pushed up to stand. He wobbled once. But Lyra was there holding his arm to help him.

He nodded his thanks but in reality he wanted to gather her in his arms and feel the warmth of her body against his. Cold had crept over him. A slow-moving dread that made his backbone quiver in fear.

Something bad was coming. And he didn't have to look down at Lyra's face on a dead woman's body to know it had something, possibly everything, to do with her.

Chapter 6

He stalked the large room from one end to the other, unable to rest, unable to stop his body from vibrating with excitement. He had wanted so much to see Caine and his team discover the body. *See* the body for what it was, and what it foretold.

The little witch must be shaking in her sensible shoes.

Grinning, he stopped at the bar in the corner of the room and poured himself a glass of blood from the open bottle. After swirling it in the crystal wineglass, he took a sip and sighed in satisfaction.

Everything was coming together just as he had orchestrated. There wasn't a move made by anyone without his knowledge or helping hand. Every murder, every scrap of evidence left at the scene, every scapegoat questioned and incarcerated was at his whim, at his mercy.

Even the dhampir's presence in Necropolis was pre-meditated. He would be a valuable asset toward the end. His father had aided him a long time ago, and now the son would be just as accommodating. He knew the man was as greedy and self-serving as his father before him.

Downing the rest of the blood in one gulp, he slammed the glass down on his large mahogany desk, shattering it into pieces. He nicked his thumb with a small shard. Dark blood pooled to the surface. Licking it clear, he swiveled around to the floor-to-ceiling windows overlooking downtown Necropolis and planned his next move. He would make sure it was one they never saw coming. One that struck fear into their hearts. Because when he finally gutted them, fear-filled blood always tasted like ambrosia.

Chapter 7

Standing out on her deck, Lyra inhaled one last breath of brisk night air before going back into her kitchen. She shut and locked the sliding glass door behind her.

Although exhaustion was settling in, she found herself restless and unable to sit still. Theron's magic still tingled on her skin, making her jumpy. She had showered the second she returned home, scrubbing her hands and arms until they were red, but his scent and magic remained.

Her stomach grumbled, reminding her she hadn't eaten since the bag of pretzels she'd grabbed out of the vending machine before going over the book with Theron. Opening the refrigerator, Lyra searched the shelves for anything to fill the void. Every shelf was empty except for some condiments, a couple of half-used jars of tomato sauce and a few Tupperware containers of leftovers transformed into science experiments. She slid open the bottom crisper and snatched the last vegetable she had in there. Celery. Not her favorite but it would do until she had energy enough to go out to her small hothouse and collect the vegetables she had growing there.

Munching on one bitter end, Lyra wandered into her living room, plopping down on the sofa. She had seven hours to shower, eat and catch a few winks of sleep before she had to be back at the lab. She had showered, now was eating, but she didn't think she could sleep.

She didn't want to admit it, but the dead body had freaked her out. However much she wanted to fight with Caine about the police protection, she was thankful for it. A police cruiser was sitting outside her house. His orders were to remain there until she went back to work. He was even supposed to follow her as she drove.

Popping the last of the celery stalk into her mouth, Lyra rested her head on the back of the sofa cushions. She needed to quiet her mind. Maybe if she had someone to talk to about everything she could turn her thoughts off and get some sleep.

"Gran? Are you there?"

Resounding silence. Eleanore obviously was still upset with her.

"I need someone to talk to."

More silence.

"Fine," Lyra huffed. "But I still talked to you even after you turned my first boyfriend into a Chihuahua."

Her answer was a brisk wind blowing through the room, rustling the green curtains at her front bay window. Followed by the *yip, yip, yip* of a small dog.

Shaking her head, Lyra laid down on the sofa. She

nestled her head onto another fluffy pillow and shut her eyes. Fatigue was taking its toll on her body. With a final thought of Theron floating through her mind like a cloud scudding through a summer sky, Lyra rolled easily into unconsciousness.

And dreamed of shadows.

She was there in Theron's dream, his *petite sorcière;* across the dark, deserted street from where he was hunkering down in the shadows, hiding from what he knew would come.

Dressed in a long, gauzy green dress, Lyra looked pale and perfect, silhouetted against the harsh light of the streetlamp overhead. He wanted to go to her, to wrap his arms around her in protection. Unable to move, he remained glued to the spot, utterly impotent.

Lyra twirled around in the glow of the light, as if waiting for someone. She seemed to be searching the shadows. Theron feared what she would see there. Nothing good ever came out of the shadows. He knew firsthand.

He saw it before she did, slithering in the dark across the cracked concrete. Eyes of red glowed in the black, causing shivers to rack his body. Had he seen those eyes before? Something about the presence seemed familiar to him. Or it could have been that he felt the same icy dread he'd felt all those years ago when he invoked that dark spell creep across him now. He'd also brought something through from the other side that day.

Turning toward the blackened street, Lyra must've sensed something approaching. Her eyes widened and, even from his distance, Theron could hear her sudden intake of breath and the quickening of her heartbeat. Fear flashed across her features.

Opening his mouth, he tried to call out to her. But his voice sounded dead, as if it had no substance to carry through the air. He tried to move, but found his limbs leaden and impossible to lift.

The thing moved out of the shadows toward Lyra. One part vampire, one part lycan in beast form and something else entirely. Something black and wet and completely alien dragged on the cement behind it as it stepped into the pool of lamplight.

She screamed and pawed at the air, trying to protect herself from the approaching creature.

Her cries for help finally prompted him to action.

Forcing his legs to move, Theron came out of his hiding spot and crossed the street toward Lyra. But it was like walking through water. Viscous and thick, the air pushed back at him as he moved—almost like swimming—to the other side.

He yelled her name. She turned toward him, seeing him for the first time and smiled, as if there weren't a disfigured creature descending upon her.

Reaching out, he tried to grasp her arm to pull her to him, to safety. An inch away, his fingertips brushed against the sleeve of her dress. He almost had her. Stretching and reaching he swiped at her arm.

He grasped nothing but air. Lyra had vanished. Only curling wisps of black smoke remained.

"No!" he screamed.

Panting, Theron bolted from sleep, sitting straight up like a board. Sweat dripped down his face and he wiped at it with a trembling hand. Reaching for the glass of water on the table beside the bed, he guzzled it down, bringing some relief to his parched throat.

Hard and painful, his heart was still thumping like a

drum. He rubbed at his chest. It felt as if his ribs were going to crack open. Taking in huge mouthfuls of air, Theron tried to regulate his breathing. Panic was very close to settling in and making a home for itself.

It had been years since his nightmares had seemed so real. Wriggling his fingers, he swore he could feel the remnants of the thick black smoke on his skin. Like tree sap, it seemed to stick to his hand in tiny black dots.

Jumping off the bed, he wandered into the adjoining bathroom and turned on the faucet. He stuck his hand under the scalding water and tried to scrub away the lingering results of his dream.

At first the dark marks wouldn't come off. It wasn't until Theron rubbed so hard that his skin came off, and he was raw and red, that the dots began to fade. Blood droplets dripped into the sink from his chafed skin.

He watched as one red rivulet swirled over the white porcelain toward the drain.

It was an omen.

Deep down inside he knew this was the face of things to come. Blood. Pain. Death. And Lyra at the center of it.

As he wrapped his hand in a cloth towel, Theron vowed that as long as he was in Necropolis he would watch over Lyra. Something was coming. Something malicious and malevolent that had its mind on the little witch.

He would do whatever it took to keep her from harm. Because he knew in some way he had helped the shadows find their mark. Because of his tainted past, he had brought them to Lyra.

He'd been such a fool to mess around with black magic all those years ago. His quest for power, especially of his own making and not in relation to his father, had blinded him to the dangers of playing with the dark, malevolent magic. At first it gave him just enough power to aid him in obtaining what he pursued—money, possessions and women. But after a time it started to demand more in payment. He'd nearly lost his soul, especially that night when sweet, trusting Jenna had been injured. He'd never forgiven himself for his negligence in performing the spell that had crippled her, and he'd been atoning for it ever since.

Lyra was his salvation in more ways than one.

Chapter 8

The next morning, as Lyra walked into the crime lab staff room, she barreled right into two hundred pounds of lycan. Luckily, Jace had lightning-quick reflexes and managed to avoid dumping his scalding hot coffee all over her.

"Whoa. Keep your eyes open when you're walking."

Lyra grunted in return and made her way to the counter to grab her morning caffeine-laced drink. She poured the dark brown liquid into a big mug and took a healthy sip. The brew was strong, bitter and delicious. It helped somewhat in chasing away the residual horror of last night's bad dreams.

She took another sip and sighed. "This is heavenly. Who made it?"

"Your Frenchie."

Her hand jerked and sloshed coffee over the rim of

her cup, sending it down to splatter on the toes of her shoes. "Excuse me?"

"Your Frenchman made the coffee. It's some blend he had imported from Colombia. I guess he had some stashed on his private jet, or something really obnoxious like that."

"He's not my Frenchie." She wiped the drips from the bottom of her cup.

"He's been here for the past two hours. He's in the analysis room with Caine going over that big old book of his."

"Oh." A sudden pang of jealousy washed over her. It was foolish to feel that way, but she couldn't help it. The translation of the book was her job, wasn't it? Why was Caine muscling in on her territory?

"You look a little miffed. Something wrong?"

She frowned. "I'm fine."

"When you said you'd bring souvenirs back from your trip, you weren't kidding." Jace smirked.

"Shut up, Jericho. Don't make me spell you again."

Jace's face fell, probably remembering the last time she used a binding spell on him. Shuffling his feet, he changed his tactics.

"Okay, I'll see you later." He stepped into the hallway and gave her a little wave. "Go find your Frenchie and get to work."

Sloshing coffee over the rim of her cup again, Lyra stuck her head out of the room and yelled at Jace down the hall. "He's not my Frenchie."

A couple of people who were walking down the hallway stopped and stared at her, making no attempt to hide the small secret grins blossoming on their faces.

Huffing, Lyra swiped at the coffee splatter on her pants and made her way down the corridor to the analysis room. She heard collective snickers as she passed. Just perfect. The last thing she needed was rumors flying around the lab about her and Theron.

Both Caine and Theron looked up at her as she marched in, chin lifted.

Setting her coffee down on the table, she looked from Caine to Theron. "Morning."

Theron kept her gaze and she could see the dark shadows under his eyes. It looked like she wasn't the only one who hadn't sleep well. She wanted to ask him what kind of dreams he had had. Had she been in them? Because he had been in hers.

The sound of his voice, screaming her name, still echoed in her ears.

Lyra!

The image of him running toward her, hand out-stretched, his face twisted in anguish, made her shiver all over again. She picked up her coffee and took a drink. The hot liquid did nothing to stem her shakes.

"How—"

"Let's dispense with the niceties and get back to the case. Okay?"

Fear clamped a hand around her heart, squeezing tight. She was afraid on so many levels she couldn't separate them into coherent thoughts. At the center of her fear stood Theron. She was scared for him, about him, and it pounded at her walls, making her feel vulnerable and out of control. She hated those feelings. It reminded her of the time she'd lost her gran, had actually watched her being gunned down in her own home by a burglar high on meth. Lyra had been incapable of doing anything about it. She hated that feeling of impotency and she never wanted to feel that way again.

Not now, not around this man who already made her weak in other ways.

Clearing his throat, Caine nodded.

She touched the book on the table. "Were you able to get any further in the translation?"

"Theron was able to decipher part of the final ceremony."

She glanced at Theron. He hadn't taken his eyes off her from the moment she'd walked into the room. His gaze was penetrating, probing even, as if searching for an answer to a question he had yet to ask.

Lifting her hand, Lyra rubbed at her mouth. Maybe she had something stuck to her lips. Maybe that was why they felt heated from his gaze. "Are you going to tell me, or do I have to guess?"

Shaking his head, he lowered his gaze and seemed to shift nervously in his seat. "Some of the symbols refer to a creature of power. The one that will open the gates."

"Our killer," Lyra stated.

Theron continued. "There is mention of the final one who will be sacrificed to the dark lord and the gates will open, giving birth to a new age on the earth." He drew a hand through his hair. "There is more about the one to be sacrificed but I can't translate it."

"Well, I think we can safely say the one is going to be female."

Caine nodded. "That's a fair assumption."

After draining the rest of her coffee, Lyra set the cup on the table and sat down. Something just occurred to her. Something making her stomach roil. "Does it clearly say the word *birth* in the text?"

Theron turned the book around and drew his fingers

over the open page of text and symbols. "Yes. *And the gate will open, giving birth to a new era*."

"What are you thinking, Lyra?" Caine asked, his eyebrow arched in that questioning way of his.

"Were any of our victims pregnant?"

Both Theron and Caine's eyes widened as the thought of what Lyra was suggesting registered.

"Interesting." Caine rubbed his fingers over the bridge of his nose in thought. Lyra could literally see the wheels turning in the chief's mind.

"Mon Dieu," Theron gasped. "You are thinking birthing a new era is a literal translation. That the sacrificed female will give birth to *le diable?* The devil?"

She shrugged. "I don't know. It's a theory."

"I'll call Givon." Caine flipped open his cell phone. "I would think if he had found anything like a pregnancy he would've told us, but I'll make sure that kind of test was done."

In silence Lyra waited as Caine talked to the coroner, and watched as Theron read over the last page he had translated. His finger traced the lines back and forth and his lips moved as he spoke the translation to himself.

She liked his mouth, she realized. It was full and sensuous. When he spoke French, it just added to the allure of it. She had to admit—even if she didn't want to—his accent sent tingles up and down her body. Where they ended in a pool of liquid heat, she definitely didn't want to consider.

Theron glanced up from reading and caught her staring at him. Blushing, she looked at Caine, who had flipped his phone shut and slid it back into his pocket.

"Givon's on it. He'll call me back with the results as soon as he gets them." Caine's phone shrilled as if punctuating his last statement. "Hmm, that was quick." He dug out his phone again and flipped it open. "Valorian."

As Caine talked, Theron reached across the table and grabbed Lyra's hand. Startled, she nearly jumped out of her chair. His touch sent heated bolts surging over her skin. "You look haunted, *petite sorcière.*"

She blushed, thankful that he mistook her look as troubled instead of heated. "I'm just tired. Bad dreams and all."

"I, too, had bad dreams." He opened his mouth to say something else but Caine was off the phone and talking before he could.

"That was Eve. She identified one of the fibers we retrieved from the body. It's vehicle carpet fiber from a Mercedes."

"That's good." Lyra pulled her hand out from under Theron's, hoping Caine hadn't noticed. But by the way he was eyeing Theron, it was obvious he had already caught it. He looked at her but didn't comment about the intimate gesture. "The matching fibers coincide with what Theron saw."

"Mahina is working on getting us a list of people who own Mercedes, particularly dark-colored ones in the city."

"I have a feeling that's going to be a long list."

"As do I," he said. "But at least it's a starting point. Other facts we found should help to narrow that down a bit."

"Like what?" Lyra asked.

"The fact that the victim worked at the club."

Lyra nearly dropped the pen she had been fiddling with. "You're joking, right?"

Caine shook his head. "I think you know me better than that."

"You know what that means," she said.

"We can't jump to conclusions," Caine said, but she could tell by the tightening of his jaw and the firming of his lips that he'd considered the possibility.

Lyra didn't like the implications of this at all. A lot of influential people frequented the club, including the mistress of the city, and their own baron, Laal. At one time, Caine had been a regular there—before he'd learned to control his vampiric urges and became comfortable with them.

"Are we heading over there to question the staff?"

Caine looked at his watch. "Yes, if we go now we can still catch the manager."

"I have heard of this club," Theron stated. "I would very much like to see it for myself."

"This isn't a tourist stop," Lyra said as she stood.

"I'll stay out of the way, but I'm going to the club either with you or without you. I do not have to answer to you, *ma chèrie.*"

Caine's lip curled. He was thoroughly enjoying their banter. "Okay. Let's go then."

Lyra glared at Theron's back as they all left the analysis room and walked down the hall to the parking garage.

Her gran's voice floated to her on a whisper.

Destiny.

"Destiny my ass," Lyra growled.

Theron glanced over his shoulder at her. "What about my ass?" He smiled.

Ignoring his question, she put her head down and concentrated on putting one foot in front of the other. Because now that he had said it, she couldn't help but stare at his butt as he walked.

Chapter 9

Lyra had been to the "club" once before. The one experience had been enough for a lifetime.

The club didn't technically have a name. There wasn't one plastered atop the elegantly carved double oak doors, or anywhere on the cream-colored linen stationery or business cards. It didn't need a name. It was enough to simply say *the club*. Everyone in Necropolis knew of its existence. It was part of what gave the undead city its unique identity.

The club was like any other high-class establishment where the wealthy could engage in a rigorous game of squash, or set out for eighteen holes of golf on world-class courses. It had a few tennis courts—indoor and outdoor—swimming and diving pools, a jogging track, a gym and a luxury spa. But for the most part, it was a place for vampires to satisfy their bloodlust in a safe and monitored environment. Other lusts were also being satisfied, but no one would come right out and admit it.

Lyra knew Caine had frequented the club for years. When she had asked him once why he still didn't go, he had said he didn't need it anymore. She supposed it had been some type of therapy for the chief. Vampires came in two groups—those who accepted their need for blood and sex as a part of their natural physiology and those who reveled in it. Caine was the former.

The club was definitely for the revelers.

When they—Lyra, Caine, Mahina and Theron— walked through the heavy oak doors, they were greeted by a beautiful vampire in a floor-length gown of red silk and jewels.

Smiling, she approached them, fangs peeking out between her lush red lips. The woman must've just eaten if her fangs were so distended. "Welcome to the club. My name is Sofia. How can I be of service to you?"

Lyra sensed a charge in the air. The talisman at her throat began to hum and vibrate on her skin. The vampiress was putting on the power. By the way Theron seemed to be enraptured by the newcomer, his tongue virtually hanging out of his mouth, Lyra could easily guess what her power was—seduction. Even Lyra could feel the beginnings of attraction in her body. Obviously Sofia had no qualms about what gender she seduced.

Mahina flashed her badge. "Can you tone it down a bit, Sofia? We're here to see the manager, not get the deluxe special."

The vampiress bristled a bit at Mahina's gruff manner, but she did dampen down her power. Enough that Lyra's amulet quieted. And she did it all without losing her smile.

"I will get Mr. Hamilton for you. Would you like anything while you wait?"

"We'll be fine, thank you, Sofia." Caine inclined his head. It was a sign of respect. Vampires were intolerably polite to each other, especially in public.

Lyra would never understand vampire politics. She knew the rules certainly, but she tried to avoid having to engage in them whenever possible. Thankfully, the vampires whom she'd call friends weren't stuffy and controlled around her.

Glancing at Theron, she wondered, not for the first time, what he'd be like without the ingrained vampire politics at play. A few times she'd seen him with his guard down and had liked it. More than was probably wise.

Mahina came back from wandering the lobby and smirked at Caine. "I can't believe you used to come here."

"It has its purposes," he replied. "Would you rather vampires indulged in their more decadent activities out on the streets?"

"Hell, no. I'd be way too busy cleaning up the damn mess," Mahina commented just as Sofia returned with a gaunt-looking man in a gray three-piece suit.

He offered his hand to Caine first since he was a vampire and the rest of them weren't. Well, Theron was half, but Lyra doubted that counted here.

"Mr. Valorian, it's a pleasure to see you again."

Caine took the man's hand, giving it a firm but quick shake. "Thank you, Bernard." He gestured to Mahina. "This is Captain Garner of the NPD, my associate Lyra Magice, and Theron LeNoir, our consultant."

Bernard glanced fleetingly at Mahina and Lyra, then his gaze settled on Theron. Smiling, he offered his hand to him. "Welcome, Mr. LeNoir. Your name is very well known to us here at the club."

Lyra frowned at Theron. "It is?"

Theron extracted his hand from Bernard's, nodding politely, and pointedly ignoring Lyra's question. "Thank you. My father speaks highly of your establishment."

Caine stepped forward in a subtle sign of authority, but it effectively blocked Theron from Bernard. "We need to speak with you about one of your employees, Lori James."

Still smiling, Bernard's gaze swept over Lyra then back to Caine. It was brief, but Lyra felt every nanosecond of it. There were nerves there. Lyra didn't have extrasensory power but she didn't need to. She was a keen observer of behavior and Bernard's was screaming anxiety. Maybe she reminded him way too much of his former employee.

"Is there a problem? Has she done something wrong?"

"Yeah, she died," Mahina huffed.

He stared at the captain for a moment as if weighing her words for hidden meaning, wondering why the lycan was speaking to him, then nodded. "Of course." He swept his arm behind him. "If you'll come this way to my office."

Lyra followed behind Mahina and Caine. Theron trailed along beside her. As they walked, she watched Theron. He kept his eyes trained forward. Not a normal behavior for someone who'd never been to a particular establishment. Usually, a person would look around, especially in a huge, lavishly decorated place like the club. The multitude of exquisite paintings on the walls alone forced a patron to stare, if not for the beauty of them then for the pure thought they must be worth over a million dollars—each.

Although his house back in Nouveau-Monde was as lavishly decorated, she sensed that he was hiding something.

"I thought you'd never been here before."

He glanced down at her, with one brow cocked, much as Caine did. "I haven't."

"Then why does that guy know you?"

"He doesn't know *me,* Lyra. He knows my last name. My father is a powerful and influential man. His name carries a lot of weight in the vampire world."

"Oh." She still thought he was hiding something.

"It bothers you, doesn't it?"

"What?"

"My vampiric roots."

Lyra scuffed her shoe on the immaculate tiled floor and nearly tripped. Theron grabbed her arm in time to stop her from landing on her face. Embarrassed, she cleared her throat.

"Why would it bother me? You're a consultant on a case, a guy who's helping me with some book translation. We're not, you know, involved or anything."

When he stopped moving, she realized that she had, too, because his hand was still on her arm. Only now was she conscious of the heat of his touch.

"Aren't we?" His thumb stroked the exposed skin on her arm. "You dream about me."

She shrugged off his touch. "No, I don't."

"You do. I know because I was there, and I saw you, too."

Lyra stared at him. She couldn't take her eyes from

his face. She saw the truth there, darkening his eyes. No wonder he had acted so strangely earlier when he had asked about her dreams. She had sensed something pass between them, a flash of knowledge, a flare of power. It was something that had only happened with one other person in her life, her maternal grandmother, Eleanore. It tied them eternally.

Did she want such a bond with this man?

"Excuse me."

Startled, Lyra swiveled around to see Caine staring at them from the doorway of an office.

"Are you joining us?"

Hands shaking, Lyra nodded and took a step back from Theron. "Yeah, I'm coming. We were just—"

"Comparing spells," Theron finished for her.

Without a backward glance, Lyra walked into the big office and slid into a vacant chair beside Caine. Theron sat down next to her.

Bernard was at the filing cabinet, pulling Lori's file, Lyra assumed. Manila folder in hand, he sat down behind the desk and opened it. "Lori's been working for us for about a year now."

Mahina flipped open her notebook. "In what capacity?"

"She worked in the spa."

"Doing what?" Mahina asked.

"Massage therapy, Reiki treatments and aura healings. Things like that."

He was holding something back. Lyra could tell by the way his gaze shifted back and forth, from Caine to Mahina to the file lying in front of him.

"Did she ever engage in the other activities that happen around here?"

Bernard leaned back in his chair. "What are you in-sinuating, Captain?"

"Oh, c'mon, Bernard. Everyone knows what goes on here. You're running a glorified sex—"

Caine put his hand on Mahina's arm, cutting off her next words. "What Captain Gardner is asking, Bernard, is if Ms. James was anyone's blood donor."

The manager glanced down at his file and flipped through the pages. "There's no one listed." He shut the folder and glared at Mahina. "If she was donating to someone outside the club, that would've been her busi-ness, not mine. But as it was, she worked in the spa and that's it."

"We'll need her client list and the schedule of the last day she worked," Caine interjected before Mahina could open her mouth, and possibly stick her foot in it.

This was another reason why Lyra hated vampolitics so much. Sometimes it stopped them from doing their jobs quickly and efficiently. A person, especially a non-vampire, had to constantly follow protocol and ask per-mission for this and that. It was exhaustive just thinking about it.

Bernard slid the file across the desk to Caine. "Is there anything else you need?"

"Yes. We'd like a tour of the spa, admittance to Lori's locker and access to the employees who worked with her."

Bernard bristled. "Can't that wait? It is Saturday, our busiest day, and we have a few very influential clients here today. I don't want to disturb them."

Caine grabbed the file, slid it under his arm and stood. "No, it can't wait, Bernard. Not unless you want Captain Garner to get angry and start a scene."

Mahina stood and Lyra had to stifle a laugh when she saw the lycan's grinning face. If there was one thing the police captain loved, it was confrontation, especially with a vampire. She disliked most of them. Caine was probably the only exception to her rule.

After a few tense moments, Bernard stood and walked to the door. "Right this way."

Lyra had the task of going through the victim's locker while Caine, Mahina and Theron got to tour the facilities and meet the other employees.

She didn't find much of anything in the small metal locker but Lori's spa uniform, which consisted of a naughty nurse–type thing, shoes and various toiletries like shampoo and deodorant. After bagging and labeling everything but the uniform, she set about going through the small pockets. There was residual magic left on the fabric. Lyra could see it as a faint red stain along the seams of the pocket.

Digging into the left slit in the jacket and then into the right, she came away with a small folded piece of paper. She set the evidence on the top of the nearest counter and took several pictures. With tweezers, she carefully unfolded it, smoothing it flat on the surface of the table. On it were initials and a time—ND 7:30 p.m.—written in red pen. After snapping a couple of pictures, she slid the unfolded paper into a plastic baggy, sealed and labeled it, setting it inside her evidence kit with everything else.

It still wasn't much to go on, but sometimes the littlest things could make or break a case. Caine had taught Lyra that among a multitude of other things when she first started with the Otherworld Crime Unit. He'd been her mentor.

Packing up her kit, she stripped off her gloves and walked out of the staff room to find the others. The hallway was devoid of any activity as she made her way to the main spa facilities. There were several closed doors along the right side. She wondered what was going on behind those doors. Perhaps the things Mahina had alluded to earlier.

Like everyone else in Necropolis, Lyra had heard the stories about what really went on at the club. Bloodletting sexual orgies. Because vampires had an oversized libido due to their bloodlust, Lyra could picture scenes like that. Wild, writhing, uncontrollable feeding frenzies.

As she thought of it, her mind conjured up an image of Theron in the midst of it. Shirt undone, fangs distended, he had the look of a man lost to his desire. A shiver ran down her spine as she tried to blink back the image. She didn't want to imagine Theron like that. She didn't want to imagine him at all, but there he was cemented in her mind, causing the first flutters of desire to build in her belly.

Angry that she couldn't stop thinking about Theron, Lyra almost missed the open doorway on her right. Stopping midstride, she glanced both ways down the hall to make sure no one was watching her. She made her way over to the gaping entrance. Rabid curiosity forced her to peek into the room.

What she saw within made her lose her breath.

A woman in a gauzy gold dress was lounging on a sofa while three men in various forms of undress serviced her. One man was on the floor at her bare feet, caressing and massaging her. Another beside her on the sofa busied himself at her breasts, licking and suckling her exposed flesh. And still another sat on her other side, his wrist to her mouth. Blood cascaded in rivulets down his arm to dribble on the sofa as she greedily drank.

Her heart pounded like a hammer as Lyra watched, enraptured by the scene before her. She'd seen vampires drink before but nothing like this. This was wild and passionate. Untamed. Purely sexual in nature. The look on the donor's face was one of utter abandon. He was lost to her completely. Lyra could see it all over him, and especially in the strain at his crotch.

She felt like a voyeur watching them, but she couldn't tear her gaze away. Transfixed, she stared as sweat trickled down her chest and back. The heat surrounding her and building inside was unbearable. While she watched, an image of Theron entered her mind again.

In her scene, he was the one on the sofa and she the one enraptured while he feasted on her blood.

Too enthralled with her carnal thoughts, she didn't feel the body pressing up against her back until it was too late.

"What are you doing?" Theron's voice whispered against her ear.

Yelping, Lyra pulled back and collided with him. Instinctively, he wrapped his arms around her as she pushed him backward into the wall.

"I didn't mean to scare you."

"You didn't," she panted, very aware of his heated presence around her, but curiously she was in no hurry to move out of it. His nearness resonated with a warmth and security. Something she hadn't felt with another living person.

She felt his elevated heart rate at her back, as well as the hardness of his body next to hers. And if she wasn't mistaken, even more of him grew harder.

"Lyra, are you all right?"

Caine's voice jolted her from her reverie and catapulted her from Theron's embrace. Smoothing out her shirt and pants, she tried to hide the pink stain in her cheeks. She hated wearing her embarrassment so prominently on her face.

"I'm fine."

"What is going on here?" Bernard asked, his voice tinged with irritation.

The doorway filled with another form—one wearing a long golden dress and a not-so-friendly look on her perfect pale face. Her long red hair cascaded around her like angry flames. "I'd like to know the same thing."

Lyra wanted to dig a hole and climb in. There was no escaping this one. She had definitely spied on the wrong vampire.

Bernard brushed past Lyra and grabbed the woman's hand in his and patted it nervously. "Ms. Devanshi, I apologize for the disturbance."

She pulled away from the manager's touch and, ignoring Lyra completely, trained a sparkling green eye on the chief. "Caine, how lovely to see you again." She offered her elegant hand.

Caine took it and brought it to his lips to press a quick kiss. "It is always a pleasure, Nadja."

"I take it you are here on business."

"Yes."

"Am I under some investigation?"

Lyra wanted to bleed into the wall behind her. Anything to disappear from the impending disaster that was about to occur.

"Of course not," Caine answered, giving Lyra a look. It was quick but she could see the irritation in it.

"Then why was your subordinate spying on me while I was engaging in my natural right to feed? In privacy."

Caine took a minute before answering. Lyra knew he was gathering his anger at the chanteuse's extreme arrogance and Lyra's stupidity for being caught. If there was one thing about Caine she had learned over the years it was his unfailing support of his team. He didn't allow anyone to treat them with disrespect.

But before he could speak, Theron took a step forward and opened his mouth. "No disrespect, madam, but the door was open. Lyra is a trained investigator, so she was merely doing her job."

Nadja arched an elegant brow and angled her head at Theron.

Lyra winced as the vampire put the power on. The temperature in the hallway actually dropped a few degrees. Oh damn, this was going to be ugly.

"Who are you to be speaking to me at all?"

"Theron LeNoir, madam." He inclined his head. "I am a big fan of yours."

"LeNoir." She smiled. "Of course, I know your father."

Lyra rolled her eyes. She should've known Theron would get out of the predicament. He seemed to have an uncanny ability to slide through the mud without getting dirty.

Nadja offered him her hand. He brought it to his mouth and pressed his lips to the back. Lingering a little too long for what was courteous, Lyra thought.

"You look just like Lucien. Handsome and refined."

"*Merci.* And you are as extraordinary as he has boasted."

Lyra had the sudden urge to rip the smug smile off the vampiress's face. Or at least toss a binding spell to permanently seal her plump lips together. If she hadn't been one of the most powerful beings in Necropolis and capable of yanking Lyra's spine through the top of her head with the twist of her bony wrist, Lyra might have considered it.

"Thank you for your understanding in this matter, Nadja. We will be leaving now, so you may return to your dinner," Caine said.

"Is this about the witch?" she asked.

"I'm sorry?"

Nadja glanced down at Lyra, and she could feel the loathing in the vampiress's gaze. "The witch who worked here. They could be twins."

Lyra's stomach roiled at the woman's words, remembering the body on the hard, cold cement. The body with her face.

"I didn't realize you knew Lori James."

"I don't."

"Then how did you know she was dead?"

"I didn't."

"You said, 'who worked here,' in the past tense."

She arched a brow and smirked. "Did I?"

Caine moved his gaze to the manager. "Thank you for your time, Bernard. We'll be in touch."

Nadja laughed. "Oh, Caine, I'd forgotten how utterly human you seem sometimes. With your questions and all. You should really come back to the club where you belong. Think of all the fun we could have together."

He tipped his head. "Good evening, Ms. Devanshi." Then, with a jerk of his chin toward Lyra, he turned on his heel and marched away. Lyra and Theron followed him.

"I hope to see you again, Theron."

Theron turned and nodded. "You, as well."

As they followed Caine out of the club, Lyra glanced at Theron, her lips pursed in thought. He noticed and looked down at her, arching one brow in question.

"Is there anybody you can't charm?"

A smile twitched his lips as he lifted his gaze from hers. "Only one."

She couldn't help the smile that broke across her mouth. With her head down and her kit swinging beside her, she wanted to tell him that wasn't true. He had charmed her.

And it hadn't taken any magic.

Chapter 10

The moment the four of them came out of the elevator to the lab, Eve charged at them from down the hall, paper rattling in her hand.

"I got the list of Mercedes."

"How does it look?" Caine asked.

"Petrifying." She shook her head, and then pointedly glanced at Theron.

Caine understood the look, and with the flair of an expert at sleight of hand, he managed to maneuver the four of them—he, Eve, Lyra and Mahina—away from Theron where they could freely talk about the case.

Lyra saw Theron's look of annoyance as he wandered away to sit in the visitors' area, but she completely understood Caine's motives for discretion. Just because he was consulting with them on the book translation, and had been to a crime scene, didn't mean he could have access to the rest of the evidence. Not for the first time, they thought someone in the lab was leaking information about the case and about the team to the media and ultimately to the killer. Months ago, when they had been working a related case in San Antonio, someone had leaked information about Caine's peculiar background to human reporters. They'd had a heyday about the fact that Caine might not have been human.

Eve continued. "There are sixty-five names on the list and half of the vampire elite are on it."

Caine took the paper from her and scanned it quickly. "Damn it. I recognize at least three members of the city council, a judge, a couple of TV personalities, Mistress Jannali's personal assistant, and our very own Laal Bask."

Mahina grinned, but it wasn't in the least friendly, more predatory in nature. "Give me half the list. I'd be more than pleased to ask the hard questions."

"If just one of these people is involved in this, we're going to have big problems. The mistress won't sit idly by and let us interrogate anyone who moves in her circle. We're going to have to handle this with care and discretion."

"Well, damn, that leaves me out. I don't own any kid gloves," Mahina grumbled.

"First things first, let's process what we retrieved from the club, get a more solid profile on our victim, and then work on this list."

"I forgot my kit in the SUV."

Eve, Caine and Mahina tried not to gape at Lyra, but she could tell their collective thought was one of shock. Lyra was usually meticulous when it came to collecting and cataloguing evidence. She was not one to forget anything—until now.

"Okay, go to the garage, grab the kit and come straight back to the analysis room so we can go through it."

"I'm sorry, Chief. I don't know—"

Caine put a hand on her shoulder. "It's okay, Lyra. This case has got us all rattled."

"I'm not rattled," she lied. "I'll be back in a few minutes."

"Take Theron with you."

She whirled on Caine. "What? Why? I don't need a babysitter."

"I know, but it will keep him occupied."

She blew at the hair hanging in her face. "Fine. Now *I'm* a babysitter."

Muttering under her breath, she turned around and started back down the hall to the garage. As she passed Theron, who had relegated himself to sitting on one of the benches, flipping through a magazine, she mumbled under her breath.

"C'mon." She gestured with her head.

Tossing the magazine onto the table, Theron stood. She could tell he was put out by the way his lips pursed together when he looked her way. "Now what corner am I supposed to sit in?"

She shook her head, ill-equipped to placate a cranky dhampir. "C'mon." She started walking down the hall.

It didn't take much for Theron to catch up with the stride of his long legs. "I don't appreciate being treated like an outcast."

"It's not personal. We can't just tell anyone the details of this case. What if it got out? What if the killer found out what we have or don't have?"

He grabbed her arm then and forced her to stop. Meeting her gaze straight on, he made his presence known. She could feel the intensity of his magic, and his vampiric allure all the way down to her toes. "You can trust me, you know, Lyra."

Trust him.

Grinding her teeth, she shook her head. "Stop talking."

Theron dropped his hand and took a distancing step back. "You are the most confusing woman I've ever met."

"I wasn't talking to you."

He glanced around. "I am the only one here. Who else would you be talking to?"

She cursed under her breath, something she rarely did. She wasn't ready to tell him that she conversed with her deceased grandmother on a day-to-day basis. Only those closest to her knew of her strange behavior. Theron already thought her to be exasperating; she didn't want him to consider her crazy, too. Talking with the dead was not a common trait, even among witches. Exasperated, she threw up her hands. "Never mind. Let's just go to the garage, get my kit and get some work done on this case."

She stomped off toward the elevator to the garage. She pushed the down button several times. The quicker this went, the better off both of them would be.

Once in the garage, Lyra marched toward the stall where the SUV was parked. She could feel Theron's presence behind her. Actually, she could always feel him, even when he wasn't so near.

She pressed the back door release on her keyless remote. There was an audible click as it snapped open.

Just as she reached for it, the sound of an engine revving reverberated all over the garage. It was so loud, Lyra had the urge to cover her ears. But she didn't get a chance to as Theron grabbed her around the waist and slammed them both into the back of the vehicle.

She was about to protest, but it died on her lips as a motorcycle whizzed by, the helmeted rider a blur of motion as he passed too close for comfort. If Theron hadn't pushed her out of the way, she might've been hit.

Turning her head, she watched the single taillight of the bike as it raced around the corner and out of the garage into the street. She knew that bike. She knew that rider.

"Kellen," she murmured.

"You know that lunatic?"

She nodded, her heart still thumping like pistons in her chest.

Theron rubbed his hands over her back. The movement was soothing, and Lyra's nervous shakes started to quiet.

"Do you think he was trying to harm you?"

She shook her head. "He's unpredictable, but I don't think he'd harm me. We've worked together for years."

As she slowed her breathing, she was acutely aware of the heat of Theron's body enveloping her. His arms were secure around her, safe and comforting. For the second time, it felt right being in his embrace, his hands caressing her back, his heart pounding in rhythm with hers.

That frightened her more than the speeding motorcycle.

"You can let me go now. Thank you for getting me out of the way."

He dropped his arms and stepped back, but she could

see the hesitation on his face before he did. "You are in danger, Lyra. Caine is right."

"Oh please, don't start." Turning, Lyra opened the back of the vehicle, grabbed her kit and slid it out. She closed the door, reengaged the lock and started across the parking lot to the elevator. "Kellen was careless. He wasn't watching where he was going. Don't read anything into it."

"It's more than that."

She met his gaze. Concern swirled in his eyes, like storm clouds.

"I can sense it."

"How?"

"I see you in my dreams, Lyra. Nightmares really. I run to you, but you disappear before I can touch you."

A shiver ran down her spine as she remembered her last dream. The one with Theron screaming her name. Could they be having linked dreams? Was the danger in her dream a reflection of what was to come? Or just a reaction to seeing her face on a dead woman?

"You're shaking." Theron neared her, stroking the tips of her hair with his fingers. "You know the dream I'm talking about. I can see it in your face."

"The dream was merely a reaction to seeing the victim that looked like me. I'm in no more danger than usual working on a case." She pulled away from his concern. Not that she didn't want him to touch her; she did with every inch of her body. But it would only complicate matters between them and with the case. She didn't like complicated. She was a simple and easy girl.

Living on her own and taking care of herself since she was seventeen had instilled a sense of simplicity. She never wanted much, never asked for much—just enough to get by without problems. Her grandmother had left everything she owned to Lyra, so it was never about money. She'd never wanted to get too involved with anyone else. Her heart had never mended after so many deaths in her family—so many she'd witnessed. Everyone left her eventually and so would Theron. It was inevitable.

But something in her heart twisted as she watched him pull into himself. His face hardened and his eyes stormed over to a gun-metal gray. "You make it very difficult for someone to care about you."

His comment stabbed her in the gut. She hated pushing him away but she knew their involvement would interfere with her job. Her goal was to catch this killer, not fall in love. Love? She shook her head, wondering how her thoughts had strayed there. She wasn't falling for him. She couldn't be.

"Let's get back." She turned from his cold gaze and dug her cell phone out of her pocket to dial Caine's number. She needed to tell him about Kellen. Something was definitely up with the vampire. He was unstable, a ticking time bomb, and Lyra had a feeling time was up.

Caine answered on the first ring. "I was just going to call you." She could hear the excitement in his voice.

"What's up?"

"Gwen's had a breakthrough. We're heading to the lab."

"We'll meet you there. Ah, I need to tell you something about Kellen."

Lyra could hear some commotion going on in the background of Caine's line. "What did you say, Lyra? I didn't hear you."

"I said there's something wrong with Kellen."

"Kellen?" There was a pause. Other voices came through the line. Raised, panicked voices. "Eve!" Caine yelled. Lyra had to hold the phone away from her ear. "Get down!"

Lyra glanced down at her phone as the line went dead. She looked at Theron. "Something—"

Everything that happened next occurred so fast that Lyra couldn't even register it as real. It was as if she were in one of her dreams.

The sound came first. Thunderous. Eardrum bursting. It reverberated from above her. Before she could recognize the sound, Theron was running toward her, his hands out, fingertips glowing blue. He was yelling at her but she couldn't hear him over the deafening explosion.

A large piece of concrete struck her shoulder. She could actually feel the bone crack under the weight as she fell to the ground.

Everything went black as the ceiling caved in on top of her.

Once the rumbling stopped and the dust settled, Theron pushed away the rock and rubble covering his legs and searched for Lyra. It was pitch-black and he couldn't see his fingers in front of his face.

Clasping his hands together, he mumbled a simple spell and a witch light grew between his palms. Slowly he pulled his hands apart and produced a glowing yellow sphere. He placed it gently on the ground and surveyed his surroundings.

He found her not far away, curled into a protective ball, bits of rock and debris scattered over her from head to toe. He had to crawl to get to her. She wasn't moving. Fear and torment pumped through his veins like rushing turbulent water. What if she were dead? Maybe he didn't get to her in time. He couldn't lose her now when he'd been so close to really knowing her, to falling for her.

When he neared, she moaned in pain, and relief surged through him, making his heart ache. Crouching beside her, he brushed the cement dust from her cheek and eyes.

"Are you hurt anywhere?"

Her brow wrinkled as she gauged herself. After a few seconds, she shook her head. "Nothing serious, I don't think."

"Okay, but move slowly."

Lifting her arm, she rubbed the dirt from her mouth and blinked up at him. "What happened?"

"I think there was an explosion. The roof caved in on us."

She struggled to sit. Supporting her under her arms, he helped her. She grimaced in pain.

"My shoulder," she said.

"A chunk of cement hit you before I could cover us with a protective layer."

For the first time, she looked around, taking in the fact that huge slabs of rock and concrete were suspended about five feet above them, as if floating in the air.

"I used that bubble spell to form a layer of air over us, like a transparent sheet of steel."

He'd almost failed to do it in time. Another minute and they both would've been crushed. He wasn't going to tell her though.

Chapter 11

She looked back at him and smiled without much humor. "That is too close for my liking."

"Mine, too." He sat down next to her, as it was impossible to fully stand.

"Thank you again for saving me." She picked some debris out of her hair.

"I'm just the right guy at the right time." He smiled, wanting desperately to soothe the haunted look from her face. Never before in his life had he wanted to take someone's pain away as he did now with Lyra. He'd take it all away if he could.

He knew she'd suffered in the past, knew about the loss of her parents and her grandmother. Although she'd treated him with disdain and put up a cold front, he saw between the cracks in her armor. He witnessed her vulnerability and instinctively knew it frightened her to the core to be so open.

He wanted—no, needed—to protect her, to save her if he had to. Nothing else mattered to him. Saving Lyra would save his own soul.

She looked at him sideways while she continued to remove clumps of rock and glass from her hair. "Yes, it seems you are." He saw her lips twitch before she looked down and brushed at her pants. She picked up a piece of burnt glass between her fingers and held it to the light. "Do you think it was the DNA lab that blew up?" Her voice caught in her throat. She struggled to keep her emotions in check.

He hesitated, unsure of what to say. He could lie to her but knew she'd see right through it and hate him for it. "It would seem that way, yes."

She tossed the glass into a corner away from them. Tears formed in her eyes. She tried to hide it by turning her head, but Theron could clearly see the liquid shimmer.

He reached for her hand and wrapped it in his. "I am sure Caine and the others are all right."

"They were heading to the lab, Theron. Gwen would've been inside already waiting for them." She sniffed and wiped at her face to hide the tears that were threatening to roll down her cheeks.

"This Gwen is a witch, *non?* Maybe she had a chance to contain herself behind a solid shield, as I did." He squeezed her hand, trying to reassure her, although he knew it was futile at best. Lyra was an intelligent woman. She knew if the explosion was forceful enough to bury them beneath tons of rubble, it was destructive enough to raze the lab or worse.

Lyra shook her head. "Gwen's a level one witch at best. Most of her power comes from her telekinetic ability."

"From what I've seen of your team, Lyra, they're

tough. They'll be okay. The best thing we need to do is make sure we're all right."

Theron took in their situation. They were quite literally buried under tons of concrete, metal pipes and other debris from the lab and offices above them. Without the bubble he had created, they would likely be dead or injured with no way to dig themselves out. Judging by the amount of debris, it would take a crew a few hours of excavating to reach their position, even after the team figured out where they were.

Lyra must've been considering the same things. "How much oxygen do you think we have?"

"Enough."

She met his gaze, seeming to stare through him. "How much?"

"Six to seven hours." He rubbed a thumb over her hand, trying to soothe the anxiety he could sense growing. "It'll be enough, Lyra. They'll find us. Caine knew we were in the garage."

She nodded, but didn't look convinced. He wasn't convinced, either.

Releasing her hand, he leaned over so he could see her other shoulder. "How is your arm?" He reached for her, but she tried to pull away. "Let me see it. I have some healing capabilities."

She turned so he could reach her shoulder easily. Carefully, he wrapped his hands around her arm, just under the socket. With his thumbs, he started to work his way up to her shoulder. She winced and tried to pull back a couple of times, but he held her in place, trying to gauge the extent of her injury.

"Your bones are not broken, but there is a lot of trauma and bruising."

"Too bad we don't have an herb garden nearby. I could whip up a healing agent to die for," she said with a cocky grin.

Theron had to suppress the urge to kiss her. She possessed a mouth made for hot kisses that lasted for days.

Unbuttoning his shirt, Theron pulled out a silver chain he always wore around his neck. On the chain was a small silver cylinder. He unscrewed the top and dripped some liquid onto his fingertips.

"What is that?" Lyra asked, wrinkling her nose.

"A helichrysum and lavender mixture I always carry with me." He rubbed the oil onto his fingertips. She watched him with a questioning look. "I have stiffness in my hands. I use it for that."

"Arthritis?"

He nodded. "Yes. I can rub it on your shoulder. It will take care of any pain you are having."

Shaking her head, but with a small smile on her lips, she rolled up her short sleeve to her shoulder. "Were you a Boy Scout or something? Always prepared."

Theron placed his hands on her upper arm and began to massage the oil into her skin. "No, never a Boy Scout. Too many boys. I wanted to be around the girls."

She laughed. "Somehow that doesn't surprise me."

He liked the sound of her laugh. It had a musical quality to it, like lively Celtic music.

They settled into a comfortable silence as he worked on her arm. Her skin warmed under his touch as he moved to her shoulder. He liked the feel of her in his hands. Her skin was soft as satin and looked like cream. He wondered how she would taste on his tongue.

He cursed at himself for thinking of her like that when she was hurt and they were both in a serious situation. But he couldn't rein in the incessant carnal thoughts he had about her. He'd been having them from the moment he set eyes on her across the crowded seminar hall.

She'd been so chaste, untouchable, before. When she had rejected him, telling him she couldn't be with him, he knew she had been right. It had not been the right time. But something had changed in the last five years. She'd changed. A sensuality he'd never felt before hummed at the surface of Lyra's skin. It was part of her, part of her energy. Even now he could feel it rippling over him, taunting his senses.

The *petite sorcière* had marked him with her magic.

After he had thoroughly massaged the oil into her skin, he sat back on his haunches and regarded her. Her face had lost the dark look. The look of someone in pain. "How does that feel?"

She shrugged the shoulder. "Much better." She smiled. "You're quite handy to have around, I must say."

He sat down facing her and rubbed the residual oil into his hands and wrists. "Handy. Hmm, can't say I've ever been described quite that way."

"No, I imagine words like handsome, charming and sexy are more appropriate for you."

"You think I'm sexy?"

She blushed. *Mon Dieu,* he adored it when she did that.

"No." She rubbed a hand over her mouth. "But I imagine lots of women think you are."

"I don't care what other women think. I want to know what you think."

"Why do you care what I think?" She frowned. "I'm just the stubborn woman who stole your beloved book."

"You are stubborn, I'll give you that." He reached for her hand. "But for all the faults you think you have, you've managed to pique my interest regardless."

She smirked. "I've piqued your interest? Well, lucky me."

"Why do you do that?"

"Do what?"

"Put this wall of hostility up every time I try to pay you a compliment or to tell you how I feel about you."

She pulled her hand from his. "I'm not hostile."

"You push back every time I try to get close."

"Maybe I don't want you closer. Ever thought of that? Maybe you're not as completely irresistible as you think you are."

He leaned back on his hands and regarded her. "Then I'd say you are a liar."

She gaped at him. "You are so annoyingly arrogant."

"I know you are attracted to me, Lyra. You try to hide it in your face but I can see it in your eyes. I can feel it on your body. Your reactions to me don't lie. You want me as much as I want you."

Her hands clenched into tight fists and he knew if she could stand right now, she'd probably punch him in the mouth and then storm away. But she couldn't, not in the concrete prison they were trapped in. He had the advantage this time. She couldn't run away from him. They would deal with this passion simmering between them once and for all.

Because if they didn't, Theron knew he'd go mad with want and desire. However odd it was to her and to him, he craved Lyra like no other woman before her.

"I could punch you right now, dhampir. You make me so angry."

"Do I?" He arched a brow. "I wonder why that is."

"I don't know. You just do."

"I think it's because I'm honest with my thoughts. While you hide yours."

"It's probably best you don't know my thoughts right about now," she grumbled.

"Hmm, don't tease me." He leaned forward and stared at her mouth. He made it known his intentions were not honorable. That he wanted—no, needed—to take her right here and now.

She gaped at him again, her cheeks going even redder. "I can't believe you're thinking with your…your groin at a time like this."

"It isn't as if we are going anywhere soon." He gestured to the cave of cement and debris entombing them.

"I'm not going to have this conversation with you."

"Why not? Do you have something better to do?"

Her eyes flashed like wildfire. "I could permanently glue your lips together with a binding spell."

He licked his lips. "Now what fun would that be? You couldn't kiss me then."

She stared at him, wide-eyed, lips parted.

"Because I desperately want to kiss you. I've wanted to from the moment I saw you again."

He could hear her heart racing just over the sound of his own. The smell of her sweat mingled with his. All he wanted to do was find solace in her. Find the peace he'd been searching for in the soft, moist warmth of her body.

"You're insane, you know that."

"I know, but I can't possibly think of a better way to celebrate that we're alive and together."

Blushing, she didn't look away and he could see his desire mirrored in her eyes.

Gripping her arm, he pulled her to him, hoping she'd see how much he ached for her. "Tell me you don't want me and I'll let you go. Tell me you don't wish for the feel of my body against yours. Tell me that and I will relent."

She closed her eyes and shook her head. "I can't tell you those things." She opened her eyes again and he saw the longing there, yet also something else. Fear. "I don't know what to do about it."

"Just give in to your desire, Lyra."

"I don't know how." She chewed on her lower lip. "I can't give you what you want."

Theron pressed his lips to the side of her mouth, lingering there, taking in her scent, and murmured against her skin. "You are what I want. Just let go."

Sighing, Lyra turned her head and found his mouth. Triumphant and alive, his heart swelled to bursting. Stroking his fingertips over her cheek, he deepened the kiss, sweeping his tongue over her parted lips.

She tasted just the way he knew she would. Like the herbs and spice that clung to her skin. Earthy, like a pagan princess. He could picture her naked, flowers in her silky hair, dancing the summer solstice in the moonlight.

He circled her neck with his other hand, lightly tracing his fingers along the slim line to the pulse thumping there. The vampire in him ached to press his tongue along the pounding vein. He'd never indulged in the suppressed urge. There hadn't been a woman before Lyra who pushed him to the edge of his desire. Once there, he would cry out for more from her. He would hunger for more than her kisses. He would crave her completely.

Content for now to just feel her blood race through her veins, Theron nibbled on her bottom lip. She returned his advances in kind, nipping and playing with her tongue and teeth.

As he moved his hands down to her shoulders and back, he could feel her vibrate under his touch. Energy sizzled on the surface of her skin. It brushed against him like a living, breathing entity. He'd had sex with a witch before, but Theron had never experienced a sensation like this.

Even as he felt the passion between them mount, he knew something was holding Lyra back. Something was battling inside her, something keeping her from surrendering to him, to their heightening desire.

To the magic that sparked all around them.

Lyra pulled away, gasping for breath. "I can't do this."

Theron ran his hands up and down her arms. Shivers radiated over her clammy skin. "Why? Have I done something wrong?"

"It's not you. You're, unfortunately, very appealing."

He smiled at her statement and her reluctance to find him attractive. That was just one of many things he found so alluring about her.

She took in a deep breath. "I'm a virgin."

Chapter 12

The moment she blurted it out, Lyra wanted to crack the invisible bubble above her head and let the concrete slabs pummel her into putty.

She was mortified. He'd probably laugh at her for being a virgin at thirty when he'd likely lost that stigma at fourteen.

He leaned back but kept her hand in his, searching her face. He didn't laugh or smile, as she thought he would. He just watched her intently.

She'd been keeping that part of her life a secret, never having told anyone before. It wasn't that she was ashamed, not really. But she felt it was too private to share with just anybody. She didn't have any close girlfriends. And the last boyfriend she'd had was a computer wizard who was more interested in creating virtual-reality spells than in her. Certainly he had wanted her in bed, but after the two times she'd declined him, he'd quit asking. This had been fine with her for the three months their relationship had lasted, because he hadn't been a man she'd wanted to make an effort for. That had been over two years ago. Since then, she'd never met a man whom she'd made an effort for.

Until now.

There was something about Theron that made her yearn for more than what she had in her life.

She shrugged. "I bet you didn't expect that little diddy."

"I didn't, but now I understand why you keep everyone at a distance."

"Is that right, Dr. LeNoir? You're a psychoanalyst now?"

"You are afraid of intimacy. Afraid of letting anyone see the real Lyra. You use that sharp tongue of yours to deflate anyone trying to get near."

She didn't like that he was analyzing her. She felt open and vulnerable. The last thing she needed was Theron poking around in her head and her heart. Already feeling flayed and stripped down, Lyra saw her anger bubbling to the surface and her defenses rising. She wasn't ready to let him in. Not yet. Maybe not ever.

"Look who's talking about intimacy. I bet you haven't dated one woman more than twice."

She saw the flash of uncertainty cross his face before he dropped his gaze. "What can I say? I like variety."

She shook her head. "You keep everyone at the surface. Afraid if they looked too closely they wouldn't like what they saw."

He smiled, but she could see that her barb had hit

the mark. His true emotions spoke volumes in the stormy centers of his eyes. "Touché. But once again you've managed to turn the conversation away from you onto me."

"Do you have to be so civil all the time?" She huffed. "Why can't we just fight like normal people?"

He lifted one perfect brow, as if his point were so obvious that she was an idiot not to have figured it out. "Because, Lyra, I don't want to fight with you. I want to make love to you."

Wide-eyed, Lyra gaped at him. His remark had caught her completely off guard. But she couldn't deny the heat spreading across her body with his bold statement.

"Is sex all you think about?"

"No, I think about other things, but not when I'm near you."

She eyed him, looking for a smirk, looking for a sign that he was joking. Because for the life of her she couldn't figure out why this man, this beautiful, elegant yet infuriating man, would be interested in her. She was plain and uninteresting compared to him. A weed to his flower. He could have any woman in the world he wanted. Why choose a prickly plain witch from Necropolis?

"Why?"

"I don't know. You're not the type of woman I usually go for."

"You mean pretty, voluptuous and empty-headed?"

He chuckled. "Any woman can be pretty. A nice haircut, makeup, fancy undergarments that nip and tuck. But you, it isn't at the surface. It comes from somewhere deeper."

She didn't want his compliments to matter, but they did. She'd never before met a man who gave them to her so freely. Infamous for seducing women, he was fluent in compliments, but for now Lyra wanted to believe he meant every single one of them.

She'd gone so long using her virginity as a shield, to keep men from getting close to her. This man in particular. But now she wanted Theron to be her first. She craved it so much her heart throbbed at the thought. But fear kept her still. Fear she wouldn't be enough for him.

"From the moment I met you something flared between us."

"It's just magic recognition," she said, trying to hide the breathy catch in her voice.

"Have you experienced this with any other witch?"

She wanted to say yes, to tell him she'd experienced it so many times it had become second nature, but she couldn't lie. Not now, not to him.

"No."

"Whatever it is, I want to explore the sensation, revel in it, completely submerge myself in it." He shuffled closer to her, pressing his knees against hers. "I know you want to explore it, too, Lyra. I can see it in your eyes. What have you got to lose?"

You, she wanted to cry out. Everyone she'd ever been close to had left her in one form or another. It wasn't always of their accord, but it didn't matter in the end. She still remained alone.

Orphaned at eleven, Lyra went to live with her maternal grandmother, Eleanore. Six years later, she'd lost her during a robbery at her gran's magic shop. Eleanore thought she could protect Lyra with her magic. She was gunned down for her trouble by a teenager hopped up on meth.

The years after that Lyra spent going to school to

study magic and criminal law—her intent being to track down and punish the boy responsible for her pain. She never found him, but instead found Caine and the rest of the crime-scene team, and formed a quasi family.

I'm still here, honey.

Her grandmother's voice echoed in her mind. Tears welled as Lyra felt her gran's presence envelop her in a phantom hug. *I know, Gran. I know.*

Wiping at the moisture with the back of her hand, Lyra said, "I've lost so much. I don't think I could handle that again."

"I'm not going anywhere."

"Not yet." She wiped at the last of the tears rolling down her cheeks. "After we translate the book, your commitment is done here. There'll be no reason for you to stay."

She sucked in a deep breath and waited for his response. Secretly, she hoped he'd tell her he had every reason to stay—and every single one of them having to do with her. She wasn't expecting a declaration of love, but she needed more than the promise of a night or two of passion. That would never be enough for her.

"Lyra, I—"

A clanging sound echoed above them. They both looked up.

Caine and Eve stared down at them, smiles plastered on their faces, relief washing over them. Caine had a jackhammer in his hands, the end tapping against the invisible protection layer Theron had invoked.

"You're both a sight for sore eyes," Caine said. "We thought we'd lost you."

Lyra pulled her hands out from Theron's and waved at them. "What took you so long?"

Relief at having been found washed over Lyra. But so did a feeling of regret. Regret that she could no longer remain here alone with Theron, trapped with no way out. It felt safe then. Safe to say what she wanted, safe to do what she'd wanted from the second she met him.

Now that moment was gone. And she wasn't sure if they'd ever get it back. Or if she really wanted to.

Chapter 13

After they were dug out from under the rubble, the whole team, including Monty, the other shift supervisor, and his people, assembled in the conference room of the NPD.

After giving both Lyra and Theron a thorough examination, the paramedics had declared that they were both without serious injuries and didn't need a trip to the hospital. Happily, Lyra's shoulder had been faring well, thanks to Theron's oil. Unfortunately, the others were not so lucky.

The crime-scene lab and offices had been ravaged. The DNA lab had been destroyed, including all the evidence from several pending cases, the equipment had been ruined and Gwen had been badly injured. She was in the hospital with second-degree burns and broken ribs.

As Lyra glanced around the conference table, she took in everyone else's injuries. Out of them all, besides Gwen, Caine was the most seriously injured. His face was cut and his arm was in a sling, having broken his wrist. Because of his rejuvenation powers, he wouldn't be in the sling long—two days max. Eve had only suffered a few minor bruises as Caine took the brunt of the explosion for her.

Theron sat next to Lyra, his book—about the only thing that survived the explosion, which was odd in itself—sitting on the table in front of him. The dhampir traced the cover with a finger, seemingly not listening to anything going on around him. But she knew he was as aware of what was going on as any of them.

"What's next, Chief?" Jace asked.

Swiveling from looking out the big bay window, Caine put his hand on Eve's shoulder. She reached up and covered it with her own. It always made Lyra ache with longing watching them together, how much love there was between them, despite all their differences.

"We need to catalog what evidence we've lost and what we have remaining. For all our cases."

There was a collective groan around the table.

"That's a lot of work," Jace commented.

"I know. I'd like you to spearhead it, Jace."

Jace glanced at his wife, Tala, sitting next to him, then back at Caine. "Why me?"

"I can help out," Monty offered.

"Thank you, Monty." Caine tipped his head at the other shift supervisor. There'd been bad blood between them, but when it came down to it they both worked for the same lab, believed in the same things—solving crime. "Could we also transfer Jace's robbery case over to one of your people for the time being?"

"You got it."

"Do you know what Gwen was going to tell you?" Lyra asked.

Caine shook his head. "No, and she's still unconscious."

"Maybe we should bring Rick in," Jace suggested. "The two of them had been working closely on this."

Lyra wanted to smile at the thought of the eager young lab technician from San Antonio. He had worked with the team on a string of murders in the city and ended up bonding with Jace and especially with Gwen when he had the opportunity to study the DNA they recovered. Ever since then, he and Gwen had been chatting online, like a couple of love-struck teenagers.

"Good idea, Jace. Call Hector and see if he can send Rick in. But make sure he doesn't tell Rick that Gwen is in the hospital. That boy's high-strung and paranoid as it is. We don't need to add to his stress."

"No problem."

"Eve's going to try to recover any data on Gwen's computer. It's fried, but she assures me if it's on there, she can find it." He smiled down at Eve.

She nodded. "Surprisingly, some hard drives can survive anything."

"Lyra and Theron will continue to work on the translation from the book as well as follow any other leads in this case." His eyes darkened. Lyra had never seen him enraged before. It was terrifying to watch. Power flowed from him, like heat waves pressing everyone back. "And I'm going to rip this place apart to find the bastard who did this."

"Do we have any ideas?" Lyra asked, trying not to shield her face from the onslaught of power radiating from him. She pitied the culprits if Caine found them first. He was usually a reserved, responsible man, but she had a feeling he'd put those things aside for five minutes with the saboteurs.

The conference door opened and Baron Laal Bask strolled in, his hair perfect, his suit and pants looking freshly pressed. It was obvious the man had been no-where near the lab when it exploded.

Snarling, Caine swiveled around. "Where the hell have you been?"

Laal smoothed down his tie. "I was in a meeting with Mistress Jannali, if you must know."

"Where?"

"Well, not that it's your business, but, at the club."

"How convenient," Jace snarled under his breath. Everyone heard it regardless. It was difficult to talk to yourself when three-quarters of the people in the room had extrasensory abilities.

Laal glared at Jace. "What is that supposed to mean, Jericho?"

"It means all hell has broken loose and you conve-niently missed it."

Laal turned on Caine. "I don't have to explain myself to you or anyone else, Valorian. As soon as I heard what happened, I rushed back here. I'm just as concerned about the damage to the lab as you are. It's going to take millions to rebuild."

It didn't surprise Lyra that the baron's prime concern was the money it would take to restore order and not the loss of evidence or the fact Gwen had been seriously hurt and could have been killed. Any one of them could have sustained a terrible injury, as well. The impact wasn't lost on Lyra that, if Theron hadn't been with her, she would've been buried beneath tons of concrete and likely wouldn't have survived.

As if privy to her thoughts, Theron reached under the table and grabbed her hand. Turning, she looked at him. He hadn't lifted his head, and was still tracing the cover of the book with his finger, but she sensed that he knew exactly how she was feeling. She squeezed his hand back in gratitude. His lips twitched but he didn't meet her gaze.

Caine closed the distance between him and Laal. "Where were you before you went to the meeting?"

"Are you accusing me of something? Because you'd better not be. I'll have more than your arm in a sling."

Lyra watched as the baron's bright blue eyes darkened to slate. Power roared off him, as well, mingling and conflicting with Caine's. The temperature in the room rose about ten degrees.

Before anyone could protest, Caine had his left hand wrapped around Laal's throat and was pushing him back into a wall. The baron raked his nails over Caine's hands, but it was pointless. Caine was the stronger vampire here. Nothing Laal did was going to affect him. The baron was completely at Caine's mercy. And by the twisted look of fury on the chief's face, he didn't have any of that racing through his veins.

"You're hiding something, Laal." Caine leaned down into the baron's face. "I can smell it on you like your cheap cologne."

"You're done, Valorian. You'll never work for law enforcement again," Laal managed to squeak out, his throat working double time under the extreme pressure of Caine's wide-palmed hand.

"Who are you covering for? It's someone at the club, isn't it?"

Lyra had no love for the baron, but she didn't like to see him being treated so harshly, especially when she didn't believe he had anything to do with the bombing. The image of Kellen racing away on his bike flashed in her mind. She couldn't keep quiet any longer. She had to say something, if only to clear her conscience.

She stood. "I saw Kellen racing away from the parking lot minutes before the explosion."

Turning, Caine loosened his hold on Laal and the baron was able to push him away. "What?"

"When Theron and I were down in the parking lot getting my kit from the SUV, we saw Kellen on his bike roaring out of the parking lot. Five minutes later the roof caved in on us."

"He almost hit Lyra," Theron added. "I had to push her out of the way."

Caine pinned Lyra with his gaze. "Why didn't you say something before now?"

"I can't believe Kellen would hurt anyone here. He's been a part of this team for years, Caine. I may not like him, but I can't believe he's a traitor or working with a killer."

"No one wants to believe that about anyone at the lab or here in the precinct, but the fact of the matter is, Lyra, we do have someone among us who is conspiring with a murderer. Every possibility needs to be considered." Caine glanced over his shoulder at Laal. "Even if that means ruffling a few feathers in the process."

Laal rubbed at his throat. "If that's an apology, I suppose I can accept it."

"It wasn't."

The baron straightened himself and looked around at the others, trying to regain his composure. "I suppose

I can be the better man here, and walk away knowing you were acting under extreme duress. I can sympathize with that, as we're all going to have our work cut out for us trying to put things back together."

Everyone ignored Laal as he continued to simper about the cost of repairs and replacing the lost equipment.

Caine nodded to Mahina. "Find Kellen and bring him in."

"Done."

"No one talks to him except me." Caine clenched his fist. "If the bastard lies, I'll know it."

"I know how to make a truth serum if you need it," Theron said, looking at Caine.

Lyra whipped around and stared at him. "That's black magic you're talking about."

"I appreciate the offer, Theron, but I don't think we'll need it. Maybe you should leave the city. You've done more than what was asked of you. I can't ask you to risk any more than you already have."

Theron's eyes raked over Lyra, leaving her feeling open and vulnerable. "I'll stay until the text and the symbols from the book are completely translated."

"Okay." Caine looked at everyone around the table. "Let's take a break for a few hours. We have a lot of work ahead of us and we need everyone to be fresh and ready to go fourteen, fifteen hours, if need be. Whatever it takes to solve this. Go home, shower, eat, sleep and be back here ready to work."

Everyone stood and started filing out of the room. Laal was the first to disappear, most likely running to a phone so he could call Mistress Jannali and tell on Caine.

Lyra grabbed Theron's arm before he could leave. "Why do you know black magic?"

Something dark and scary crossed Theron's face. "It's a long story and one I am not willing to share."

Lyra's hand fell away. Her stomach rolled over at the icy timbre of his voice. She knew Theron had secrets. Now she wasn't sure she wanted to know them.

"I'm going to my hotel and taking the book with me. We can work while we eat."

"I'm not hungry."

"Why do you have to argue about everything?"

"I'm not."

"Then don't be foolish. You're hungry, hurt, and we can work while I fix your shoulder." He turned to leave. "I'll grab the book. Meet me outside."

As she watched him go, her hands began to shake. There was something innately dangerous about Theron. She'd only glimpsed it, but it was definitely there. Could she trust him?

Glancing at the ceiling, she said, "Little help here."

Trust your heart.

"What does that mean, Gran? Why can't you just tell me what to do?"

I don't want to interfere.

"What? Where was that attitude when I was a teenager and I wanted to go to that all-night concert in Vegas?"

I can't tell you what to do, my dear. There are some things you have to figure out on your own.

She threw her hands up in defeat. "Great, but I have no idea what that is."

Her heart told her she could trust Theron, but her head screamed at her that something was wrong. And finding out would risk something more than she was willing to give, the one thing her grandmother had told her to trust—her heart.

Chapter 14

From the front seat of his car, he had watched the witch and her dhampir go into the hotel. Oh, what he wouldn't give to go into the room and finish his work. But the timing was off. There was still one more to go. One more work of art he needed to create.

The wait wouldn't be long now. Everything he had planned from the beginning was coming to fruition and soon he would reap the rewards of his labors. He could almost taste the final act on the tip of his tongue. Like a fine wine, it lingered on his flesh with its sweet after-bite. Soon, he promised himself. Soon he would have it all and rule without question, without humanity's morality dictating his actions. He had lived long enough like that among them, pretending to be something he wasn't.

He hated them all for the facade he had to put up. It sickened him to have to pretend. He wanted the world to know his true purpose, his true identity, and wither in fear of his power.

Already people bowed down to him, did his bidding without a clue as to his true identity. What would his followers do once they found out who he really was? That he had tricked them all. Would they rejoice in his tremendous supremacy or quiver in the face of his terrible beauty? He hoped it would be both.

Once he accomplished his ultimate task, his first order of business would be to eliminate most of his followers, sniveling, greedy creatures that they were. But he would reward a rare few who had proved to him they were worthy to serve him in the new world.

Grinning, he thought of one such creature who had served him well for years. He had a special treat for her. His body quivered at the devilish torments he had in store for her. By the end, she would both loathe him and love him. Right before he cut out her heart and ate it. For one as cruel as she couldn't be trusted to keep around.

No, he was of the sound mind of keeping his enemies close and eating his friends.

Chapter 15

Theron's suite at the hotel was bigger than her house, but Lyra was too worn out to care. She collapsed on the sofa while Theron went into the bedroom to get more oil from his luggage. The first application was wearing off and her shoulder was starting to ache. The pain traveled over her collarbone and up to her jaw. She could barely open her mouth without a twinge of pain zinging through her. Some might have thought that was a good thing, considering her penchant for speaking her mind.

Resting her head on the back of the luxurious sofa, Lyra closed her eyes. She felt like she could sleep for a week. Both her mind and her body were exhausted.

Her eyes snapped open the second Theron nestled in beside her on the sofa, his hands already probing her arm.

"You should sleep," he said as he massaged the ointment into her upper arm.

"So should you."

"I can't sleep when I'm this tired."

"Neither can I." She smiled at this shared quirk. She wondered what other things they had in common. She'd been so busy battling her attraction to him that she had never bothered to find out more about him. Maybe they were more alike than she wanted to acknowledge.

As his hands moved over her skin, caressing and massaging her shoulder, Lyra watched him. She surveyed his face, taking in every nuance, every gorgeous feature. Sometimes it hurt to look at him. He was captivating with his stormy gray eyes, long black eyelashes, high cheekbones and full, sensuous lips. It was as if he had been cut from a piece of white granite, all hard planes and smooth surface.

Letting her eyes travel down past his mouth, she wondered how chiseled he was beneath his shirt and pants. From the way he moved, it was not hard to imagine that he possessed unbridled strength. He exuded the grace most vampires had, screaming power and precision. Lyra had always thought Caine exemplified the ultimate vampire allure, but since meeting Theron she'd had to amend that thought. Theron was the epitome of vamp seduction.

Finishing slathering the oil on, Theron leaned away from Lyra. He used a white cotton towel to wipe the ointment from his hands. "I suggest you close your eyes, Lyra. Your thoughts are easily read."

As if waking from a trance, Lyra shook her head and noticed that Theron was staring at her, his eyes dark, his lips parted. Restrained desire tightened his jaw.

"I thought you wanted to, you know, have me."

His nostrils flared. "I do, but now is not the time." He stood and marched into the bedroom.

Exasperated, she let out an angry sigh. "Oh, and after nearly getting buried under tons of cement was a good time?"

He strode back into the room carrying an unopened bottle of water. After unscrewing the cap, he handed it to her and sat on the chair opposite her. "No, it wasn't, and I apologize."

Refusing to take a sip, she set the bottle on the glass coffee table. "It's because of what I told you, isn't it?"

"It is more than that."

"I thought doing a virgin is a big deal for men like you. You know the whole deflowering thing." Frustration and shame fueled her words.

"What do you mean, men like me?"

She could plainly hear the anger in his voice. She didn't care. Maybe if they fought, maybe if she made him angry enough, she'd stop the yearning in her heart and body. The constant battle between desire and logic was draining her. She was tired of battling it. To keep her mind intact, one half had to be victorious. At this point she didn't really care which one.

"It's no secret you've slept with a lot of women. Having a virgin I thought would be, you know, cool."

"For such an intelligent woman, you can be extremely dumb sometimes."

"You're calling me dumb?"

He nodded. "You claim to be a good crime-scene investigator, yet you've convicted me without any evidence." He arched his brow and leaned back in the chair, affecting an air of ambivalence, but Lyra could see him seething at the edges. She had hurt him with her cavalier assessment of his character. "You know little to nothing about me to make such judgments. I've never disrespected you, Lyra. I'd appreciate it if you afforded me the same courtesy."

Embarrassment crept over her. She had unfairly judged him. She had spent enough time with him to know he was layered with contradictions. He'd seemed haughty when he first arrived in Necropolis. But the day at the crime scene she'd seen sorrow and anguish on his face when he had to touch the victim. It was obvious he had a conscience and a sense of remorse.

Also, he'd saved her twice from being hurt. The last time he had saved her life. Would an ambivalent man with an uncaring heart have done that? Would he have treated her with such care and concern by healing her shoulder?

She sighed and rubbed a hand over her face and through her hair, which she just now realized was a mess. "You're right. I'm sorry, Theron. I've treated you with nothing but disdain from the beginning." She shook her head at her own prejudices. How many times had she lectured Jace about his prejudices toward humans, and here she was coming to the same conclusions about Theron? "I don't feel that way about you. I think that, um, you're a good man."

He stared at her, silent, brooding, for what felt like an eternity. She fidgeted in her seat, nervous under his scrutiny. Finally, he spoke. "I accept your apology, Lyra." He gestured toward the bottle of water on the table. "Now drink. It's healing water. It will help with your shoulder."

Letting out the breath she hadn't realized she'd been holding, Lyra picked up the cold bottle of water and took a sip. The icy liquid soothed her parched throat and she drank more.

As she set the bottle back down, something on the label caught her eye. Something written in dark purple calligraphy. She held it up to her face and read it over. And then again.

"Where did you get this?" She turned the bottle around so he could see the label.

"I asked the front desk this morning to bring me some. I always like to have it around, just in case. Why? Is it not good? Did they bring me plain bottled water?"

"No, it's healing water all right. But it's from New Destiny."

He arched a brow. "Is that not a good place?"

"I should've made the connection." She tapped herself on the forehead with her thumb.

"What's the connection?"

"I found a folded piece of paper in the victim's spa uniform. It said ND—7:30. I thought it was someone's initials, but maybe it's a place." She held up the bottle. "New Destiny. ND. It's a magic shop. Not one I go to as it caters to those swimming in the gray areas of magic usage."

Theron's lips twitched into a grin. "Not so dumb after all."

She returned his smile. It felt good to share this with him. She wondered what other things they could share. If only he wasn't leaving. "I have my moments."

"*Oui,* you most certainly do."

She stood. "Okay, let's go. I'll drive."

"First we eat, then we will go."

"Theron, we don't have time—"

He stood seconds before there was a knock at the

door. "Make time, Lyra. You can barely function." He walked to the door, opened it to let the porter wheel in the room service tray. The delectable smells made Lyra nearly swoon with hunger. Once the porter left, Theron lifted the lid on the food platter. "Eat. Then we will follow this lead."

Inspecting the variety of food on the tray, Lyra said, "We?"

Theron smiled and plucked a piece of fruit from one of the platters. "Someone once told me I was handy to have around. I'm with you on this, *petite sorcière,* to the end."

She took half a cucumber sandwich and bit into it. She was pleased that he wanted to stick with her through this. She'd never really had a partner of sorts. On some cases Jace and she would work together, but most of the time she worked solo. She preferred it that way. Until now. His presence alone made her feel safe and secure.

How would she feel when he finally had to leave?

Chapter 16

New Destiny was downtown at the corner of Digger and Third Avenue, a few blocks away from a vampire blood bar called the Red Express. The magic shop catered to those teetering on the edge of the black. It was illegal to practice the dark arts, but Lyra knew there were witches who did it anyway.

She'd been on a few cases where people had been murdered by nefarious spells. Sometimes premeditated, sometimes not. Witches ended up killing by accident because of their ignorance of the evil intent of black magic. Ignorance was no excuse.

Coils of patchouli-scented smoke greeted Lyra the moment she pushed open the front door. In some circles, patchouli was known as Graveyard Dust and was supposedly used in demon summonings. But Lyra knew of regular people who used the incense to cover other smells, like cannabis. When she was in college, her roommate had used it often. Ever since, Lyra had hated the odor. It gave her a headache.

The bells hanging from the ceiling chimed as Theron, then Tala, followed through the door, letting it shut behind them. They both wrinkled their noses at the pungent odor.

"I hate this smell," he said as he trailed behind her through the dimly lit shop.

"Me, too." Tala wiped her nose, most likely trying to remove the offending smell from her powerful lycan olfactory cells.

Before Lyra and Theron had left the hotel, Lyra had called Caine to tell him what she had found and where she was going and to send an officer to make it all aboveboard. Mahina had been occupied tracking Kellen down, so the chief sent Tala. Lyra didn't mind. She liked the half lycan and she was proving to be a really good cop in Necropolis.

As Lyra moved through the store, she took in the sur- roundings. The store was like most other magic shops— even her gran's shop. Shelves of candles, crystals and essential oils lined the walls. The more valuable items, like athames, chalices and mirrors, were near the front counter in glass display cases. Robes and capes hung on hangers in the corner near a full-length mirror on the wall. Some witches prided themselves on looking styl- ish while practicing their craft.

Lyra couldn't have cared less. She brewed most of her spells at home in a pair of cotton shorts and a ratty old T-shirt. Easier to clean up if a spell went bad and exploded all over the kitchen. The one and only time she'd worn a ceremonial robe was to her gran's wake.

Eleanore's essence surrounded Lyra as it often did when she was thinking about her. Her jasmine scent perfumed the air. Lyra inhaled deeply, drawing strength from her gran's presence. But something was off. Lyra could sense that Eleanore was agitated and unnerved.

Lyra stopped walking and frowned. "What's wrong?"

Nothing, darling.

"Gran, I can tell when you're upset."

Theron came up beside her. "What did you say?"

Lyra glanced around the store looking for something amiss or out of place. Was there danger here?

Theron touched her shoulder, concern furrowing his brow.

She smiled at him and continued toward the main counter. "Everything's fine."

When they neared the long wooden counter at the back of the store, a woman appeared from behind the beaded curtain. She looked like a stereotypical witch with long black hair, streaked by gray, and wearing a long, flowing, flowery dress and sandals. The one main difference about this witch was that she had some psychic ability. Lyra could see it glow around her like a halo. Gwen had the same type of shine.

She smiled brightly as they approached. "Good evening. What can I do for the NPD?"

Tala glanced down at herself and her jeans and T-shirt. "Is it that obvious?"

The woman chuckled. "Yes. Your aura is practically exploding with browns and blues. Authoritative colors."

"I'm Officer Jericho." Tala flipped open her wallet to show her badge. "This is Lyra Magice from the crime lab and Theron LeNoir. Could we have your name?"

"Claire Mitchell." She sat on a stool behind the

counter and picked up a large piece of quartz, juggling it between hands.

"Are you the owner of New Destiny?"

"Yes."

Lyra stepped forward with a picture of the deceased. "We have some questions about a woman named Lori James. Did you know her?"

Claire glanced down at the photo then smiled at Lyra. "I knew of your grandmother."

"I'm sorry?" Lyra flinched.

"Eleanore Sowards from Las Vegas. She had a shop called Wind in the Willows."

"Yes, that's right." Lyra's hands began to shake. Dread washed over her like a wave of dark water. "Did you know her well? I think I would've remembered you from the wake."

"No, I didn't know her personally." Claire smiled again, then set the quartz down on top of the picture of Lori James. "You look just like her."

"Excuse me?"

"Lori." She tapped the edge of the photo on the counter with her index finger. "You could be her twin."

It felt like the world was tipping and Lyra had to brace herself on the counter. A rush of dizziness spread over her. She had to blink back the black spots in her eyes; she feared she'd get sick.

Feeling a solid presence next to her, Lyra glanced sideways and met Theron's gaze. He touched her arm, holding her lightly but solidly on the elbow, keeping her from buckling at the knees. Tala had also moved alongside her. The lycan's heat register had gone up a few degrees. It was obvious that her temper was rising at the woman's evasiveness.

"Did you know Lori James or not?"

Claire nodded. "Yes, I know her. She comes here to shop."

"When was the last time you saw her?"

"Three days ago maybe."

"Daytime, evening?"

"She always comes in during the evening, right before I close at eight." Claire regarded Tala then Lyra. "She's dead, isn't she?"

"Yes," Lyra answered, still unable to shake off the heebie-jeebies that were coursing over her. But she had a job to do. Questions about her grandmother would have to wait. "The last time you saw her, was she with anyone, or did she talk to anyone in your shop?"

"She was alone and, if I remember correctly, there was no one else in the store."

Disappointment curled in Lyra's gut. She had hoped this would lead them somewhere, to another clue. It did establish a time line, which was helpful, but as usual she wanted the one thing that would crack the case. She desperately wanted to solve this one. Maybe then, she could erase the thoughts of her own death from her mind.

"Can you remember what she bought? Anything out of the ordinary?"

"She bought some candles and oil. Rose oil, I believe." Claire's brow wrinkled. "Now that you mention it, she did buy some vervain leaves and a smudge stick."

"Was she moving, I wonder? Smudge sticks are used to cleanse new places."

Tala flipped open her phone. "I'll call Mahina. She was at the vic's apartment. Maybe there were boxes packed up." She stepped away to make the call.

"Vervain leaves are used to ward off unwanted attention, aren't they?" Lyra mused. "A witch could make a charm to, say, stop her ex-boyfriend from calling her or coming to see her, couldn't she?"

Claire nodded.

"Vervain is also used in protection spells," Theron added.

Lyra eyed him. "Protection from what?"

"Demons."

Claire snorted. "You don't honestly think that Lori was involved in the black."

"What do you know about the dark arts?" Lyra asked her, sure that the woman was not as innocent as she seemed. There was something about her that read wrong.

"Enough to know that when you play with the devil, you're going to get burned." Her gaze swung to Theron and she grinned. Lyra noticed that her front tooth was chipped. "Isn't that right, Monsieur LeNoir?"

Theron bristled at the comment, his eyes darkening in anger. "Do you know me, madam?"

"No, but I can see you quite clearly."

Tala returned to the counter before Lyra could comment. Something had transpired between Theron and Claire, something she wasn't sure she really wanted to know.

"Mahina said there was no indication that the vic was moving. No evidence of a boyfriend at the apartment, either." Tala looked from Lyra to Claire then to Theron. "What's going on?"

Theron shook his head. "Nothing of consequence."

"Is there anything else you can tell us, about Lori's last visit to your shop?" Tala asked.

"No, I'm sorry. Nothing comes to mind. She bought her things then left, getting into her car out front."

Lyra frowned. According to the vic's records, she didn't own a vehicle. "What kind of car?"

Claire looked past them toward the big bay window facing the street. "A dark-colored sedan of some sort." She shook her head. "I don't know cars, so I couldn't tell what make it was. But it definitely had four doors and was a dark color."

"Do you recall if she opened the driver's-side door or the passenger side?"

Lyra glanced behind her at the street through the window. All the cars parked along this side of the street were pointing east; therefore, if Claire actually saw Lori get into the car, she saw her get into the passenger side.

"Passenger side."

Tala nodded as she wrote down all the info in her notebook. "That's good. Thank you, Ms. Mitchell. You've been very helpful."

Claire smiled at Tala. "I'm glad I could help." Then her gaze moved to Lyra. "I must talk to you before you go."

"I'm listening," Lyra responded, that sense of dread surging over her again.

"Alone, my dear. The things I must tell you are for your ears only."

Theron squeezed her arm. "We should go back to the lab. There's a lot of work still to be done."

Theron must've shared her sense of dread, as his hands shook slightly and were slick with sweat. There was definitely something about the woman that didn't resonate well with any of them. Tala also looked weary.

But Lyra wanted to know what this woman had to say. Psychics were a strange bunch, but they could more times than not tune into something that ordinary people couldn't see or hear.

Lyra nodded and Claire led her to the back room behind the beaded curtain.

A small table and two chairs were arranged in the corner. The smell of patchouli was strongest back here. This was where Claire must've done readings, as it was obvious the woman had some ability. Lyra had sensed it the moment they walked into the shop.

Claire sat in one of the chairs and gestured for Lyra to sit in the other. Once Lyra was seated, Claire set her hands on top of the table, palms up. It was an unspoken invitation for Lyra to give Claire her hands to read.

She didn't want this woman to touch her, but she needed to hear what Claire had to say. Although Lyra knew deep down inside, in the place that held her magical ability, she wasn't going to like what she heard.

Claire held Lyra's hands lightly, her fingers barely curling over, and stared into Lyra's eyes. The woman had big brown eyes, the kind a person could easily get lost in. Now they seemed to see right through Lyra, as if she were made of glass.

"I see death surrounding you."

Lyra smirked. "I'm a crime-scene investigator. That's part of the job."

"It sticks to you like gossamer threads."

Shivering, she had the urge to swipe at her arms and legs. Maybe it was the power of suggestion, but Lyra felt as if she needed a shower—that something was clinging to her skin.

Claire wrapped her fingers around Lyra's hands and squeezed tight, pulling her forward on the table. "You are in danger."

"From who?"

She shook her head. "It's not clear, but I see a great betrayal and heartache."

Instantly, Lyra thought of Theron. A man with secrets. A man she suspected possessed a dark past.

"Someone close to you has the black mark on them. Take care in your trust. Misplace it and you will suffer greatly." After her last word, she released her hold on Lyra's hands and sat back in her chair.

With a brisk nod, Lyra stood on shaky legs and turned to make her way out.

"Say hello to your grandmother for me, will you?"

Swiveling around, Lyra eyed Claire cautiously. The woman smiled at her in that knowing way and waved her hand to dismiss her. Swallowing down the bile rising in her throat, Lyra pushed past the beaded curtain and back to where Tala and Theron still stood waiting for her.

As she moved near Theron, he regarded her warily. She could sense that he was trying to figure out her mood. Did he sense that the psychic had revealed something about him? What about his past did he hide so deep?

"Are you okay?" he asked.

She nodded and moved past him. Uncertainty swirled in her head and made her stomach roil. She hated that she harbored suspicions about Theron. But they were there, needling her head and her heart.

She desperately wanted to trust him, but there was too much he wasn't saying. Too many secrets stashed away. Had he come to Necropolis for another reason? She didn't even want to consider it.

Trust him, Lyra.

Eleanore's voice echoed in her mind and Lyra shook it loose. *I can't. He has too many secrets.*

There was no response.

Chapter 17

"Someone's been snooping around." Theron paced his hotel suite as he listened to Henri, his aide, on his cell phone. Right after they left New Destiny, he got the call from his assistant. Sensing the importance of the call, he had asked Lyra to drop him off at his hotel. She had looked at him strangely, but didn't comment. He was thankful for that.

"Caine Valorian more than likely talked to Inspector Bellmonte about my work with the police."

"It's more than that, Theron. There have been calls to the museum curator about some of your collection pieces, and attempts have been made to collect information about your bank accounts."

LeNoir was a powerful family name, so it didn't surprise him that inquiries were being made about him. But his bank accounts? That seemed a little more unsettling than anything else.

"What are you thinking, Henri?"

"It smells like blackmail," his young aide said.

The thought had crossed Theron's mind. There had been a blackmail attempt on him years ago by a money-hungry young witch trying to capitalize on the LeNoir name and Theron's goodwill. It had been solved, thankfully, without any payment.

"Would anyone there have any reason to do this?"

"No," Theron replied. "I don't personally know anyone here. My father, on the other hand, is very well acquainted with some of the more influential citizens."

His thoughts strayed toward the very enchanting chanteuse Nadja Devanshi. It had been obvious that she knew Lucien personally, possibly even intimately. His father was known to have several mistresses, even when he was still married to Theron's mother. Did she know something about his father that she could use against Theron? Maybe. The way she had looked at him had been unnerving—as if she could see the black marks on his soul.

"I'll phone Lucien in the morning," Theron said, already dreading the call. He didn't get along with his father. Once he had respected the man, but after certain events, Theron chose to sever their relationship. He preferred to discuss family matters over the phone, instead of in person.

The vampire frightened him.

"I doubt he'll shed any light on it, but if I tell him someone's sniffing after the family money, it'll prompt him to some kind of action."

"I'll keep an eye on things here, sir. If I see anything else irregular, I'll call you right away."

"Thank you, Henri."

Theron flipped his phone closed and set it on the

glass coffee table in the living room. Uncorking the bottle of wine he had brought with him from France, he poured a glass and sat on the sofa. Fatigue was starting to worm its way in.

He'd been on the go since touching down in Necropolis a day and a half ago. He hadn't had a decent night's sleep since the vivid dreams about Lyra began. She even plagued his waking thoughts. He couldn't seem to exorcise her from his mind.

He gulped down the wine, hoping it would dull his senses. Maybe then he would stop smelling her on his skin and clothes, hearing her voice in his head, and remembering how she'd looked at him after a few private words with the psychic.

She had definitely regarded him differently after stepping through the beaded curtain. Warily. As if she'd been told he was keeping secrets from her.

Cursing, he ran a hand through his hair. He was keeping secrets, but it was for her own good. She didn't need to know about his past. It would only hurt her. And yes, ruin any chance of them getting together.

He wanted her desperately. Even after she had told him that she was a virgin, more so probably. To be her first would be an honor. To show her the beauty of her body, and open her to so many sensual delights—she'd go mad with desire. He couldn't deny it. He wanted to make Lyra scream his name, to ache for him even after they had done the deed. He wanted her to remember him as being the beacon of passion during a dreadful time.

For once he wanted to be associated with the light instead of the dark.

After pouring another glass of wine, Theron flipped through the big book on the table to the last page he and Lyra had worked on. They were so close to figuring it out.

This time something caught his eye. An innocuous symbol. It was almost hidden among the others. But something about it registered with him. It looked like an *M* with a loop after it. Very unassuming, but put into context it had meaning. Grave meaning.

Hands shaking, he opened a file in his laptop. He had extensive symbol catalogs on his hard drive. This one held archaic symbols and text used in black magic. At one time, he had been very familiar with them. He had utilized them extensively in spells and incantations until that night when everything had gone wrong.

He scrolled down to the end of the alphabet and stared at the zodiac sign for the Virgo. A letter *M* with a loop behind it. He glanced back at the book. The symbols were too similar for the resemblance to be ignored.

Why Virgo? What did that have to do with sacrifice?

Rubbing the bridge of his nose between two fingers, Theron closed his eyes and tried to think, tried to reason through it. Then, like a sledgehammer in his mind, the answer came to him. Dread surged through him at the thought. Most of the text had been written in an odd mix of Latin and Aramaic. *Virgo* was the Latin word for "virgin."

Whoever was summoning demons needed a virgin for the final ceremony to be used as a Virgin Mary–type of vessel for the next evolution of evil. The portal for something evil to come through.

Lyra was to be that sacrifice: she was to give birth to a demon.

Theron felt sick. Maybe he was jumping to conclusions, but to him it made sense. He had experience in the dark arts. Simple logical spells were twisted and molded to suit the dark practitioner's purpose. At one time, he himself had harbored those immoral purposes. He had practiced with greed in his heart and soul.

Grabbing his phone from the table, he flipped it open and prepared to dial Lyra's number. But his finger froze on the keypad. A rush of selfish thoughts invaded his mind.

He snapped the phone closed. Sighing, he leaned back against the sofa and shook his head. He couldn't tell her. She would wonder how he had figured it out.

And what if he were wrong? He'd be tipping his hand even before he knew the stakes. He couldn't take the chance until he was one hundred percent certain. He didn't want to risk losing Lyra before he'd even had a chance to get to know her.

Instead, he would stick close to her to make sure no harm came to her. If she were indeed the target, Theron would be there to catch the killer. He would do whatever it took to keep her safe. He would use whatever means he had at his disposal. Even if that meant risking his soul all over again.

Lyra returned to the precinct alone. After a cryptic phone call, Theron had asked her to drop him off at his hotel. She was glad for the reprieve from him; she needed time to straighten out her feelings.

As she marched toward the conference room reserved for the crime-scene team, Eve snagged her in the hall. She could see the flush of excitement on the human's face. Something must've happened.

"Mahina brought in Kellen," Eve said, as she pulled

Lyra by the arm toward one of the interrogation rooms. "Caine's questioning him now."

The whole team was assembled outside the viewing window, watching as one of their own was interrogated. Lyra stood beside Eve and swallowed hard. She hated seeing Kellen in the room.

Kellen was seated, leaning back, arms and legs crossed, looking unaffected and bored. Caine sat on the edge of the table near Kellen, looking calm and reserved. But they all knew otherwise. The chief was likely seething inside, but he was a vampire and possessed an unnatural air of detachment in extreme circumstances. Most times, he seemed aloof and cold, but deep down the team knew he was one of the most compassionate people on earth.

Lyra glanced at Eve, who knew that fact more than any other person.

"It's killing him to have to do this," she said, never taking her eyes off her husband.

"I know," Lyra responded, but this wasn't the first time Caine and Kellen had had it out. Not long ago, Kellen had been flippant about Eve's kidnapping. Caine had nearly snapped his neck over it.

"Are you going to tell me what this is about, Chief? There's a hockey game on. The Canucks are playing," the group could hear Kellen say.

"Where were you between ten this morning and two in the afternoon?"

Kellen smirked. "Are you kidding me?"

"Answer the question."

Kellen lifted his gaze to meet Caine's. Lyra imagined that the temperature inside the room was either dropping or rising, depending on whose power was more dominant at the moment. Caine was the stronger vampire, but Kellen had his ways. She'd once seen him crush the barrel of a handgun in one hand.

"In my designated cage, running ballistics on the Jenson robbery."

"Was anyone with you?"

"I was alone, as usual. You know that's how I work."

"Were you ever in the DNA lab between those times?"

Shaking his head, Kellen leaned back in his chair, rubbing his fingers over his chin. "I can't believe you'd think I had anything to do with blowing up the lab."

"Were you in the DNA lab between those times?" Caine asked, his jaw rigid as he spit out the words again.

"Yes, I was talking to Gwen."

"At any time, did Gwen leave you in there alone?"

"No," Kellen said equally as rigid. "You can ask Gwen."

"I would, but she's still unconscious."

Kellen exploded out of his chair and rushed to the window that the team was watching him through. Of course he knew they were there. It wouldn't have surprised Lyra if he could actually see them as clear as water. "Screw this, man. I didn't blow the lab up."

Caine stood, but didn't move away from the table. "Why were you racing away from the parking lot minutes before the bomb went off?"

Kellen swung around. "What?"

"Lyra saw you racing out of the parking lot on your motorcycle minutes before she was nearly buried alive under tons of concrete."

Lyra backed away from the glass as the vampire turned and looked right at her. Her heart was hammering hard in her chest and she could hardly breathe.

Lifting his hand, he finger-waved at her.

Eve glanced at Lyra, a look of worry creasing her brow. "Can he see us?"

"I don't know."

"He's just screwing around," Jace said. "Trying to intimidate us."

Caine slammed his hand down on the metal table, bowing it in the middle. Everyone jumped, except Kellen.

"Answer my damn question, Kellen. Someone could've been killed today. Gwen was seriously injured and we lost almost all our evidence in this case and several others. Why can't you just be straight with me?"

"Because you're not being straight with me, Chief. This is about more than just me racing away from the scene of the crime."

"Okay." Caine leaned on the table with his fist. "You've been seen at the club a lot lately. I also heard that you were friendly with Lori James, our latest murder victim."

Jace cursed. "Why didn't Caine tell us any of this?"

"Maybe he just found out himself," Lyra answered. But she, too, didn't like that the chief had kept that information to himself.

Turning, Kellen returned to the chair and sat down, crossing his legs casually. The look he gave Caine was not casual at all.

"Yes, I knew Lori. As did most of the clientele. She was a very friendly girl, if you know what I'm saying."

"You should've come to me right away with this, Kellen."

"I know, but I'm not proud of my frequent visits to the club." Kellen rubbed a hand over his head, and then sighed.

"You've never been one to shy away from the baser traits of vampirism. Why the change?"

Kellen crossed his arms in defense and avoided Caine's intense gaze.

Caine slammed his hand on the table again. "Tell me what the hell is going on, Kellen."

Without looking up, Kellen sniffed. "It seems that I have SC."

Lyra gasped and Jace swore. They both knew what that meant for Kellen. Now his erratic behavior made more sense.

"I've been trying to flush it out with extra blood, but so far it hasn't worked."

"What's SC?" Eve asked.

"*Sangcerritus.* It's a rare blood disease vampires can contract. The literal translation is 'crazy blood.' When it's full blown it can drive the vampire mad." Lyra felt guilty now for considering that Kellen could do such a heinous thing as blow up the lab. He was sick, not a traitor or a conspirator.

Sighing, his anger defusing, Caine slid back onto the table. "Why didn't you tell me?"

"Because I knew you'd have to put me on a leave of absence." Kellen shook his head and let it fall back. "I love my job, Chief. I don't have anything else."

"How long have you had symptoms?"

"Six months at least. Maybe more. I was trying to hide it—even from myself." He sighed again. "I had just talked to my doctor on the phone before I wheeled out of the garage. I didn't see Lyra. I was too messed up to see much of anything."

Caine nodded then stood. "I'm going to need you to give a statement to Mahina about knowing Lori James and your whereabouts during the explosion."

"Yeah, I figured as much."

Caine started for the door.

"Oh, hey, this might interest you," Kellen said as he sat up in the chair. "Guess who frequently fed on Lori's blood?"

"I'm listening."

"Your favorite singer. What's her name? Nadja something."

Lyra sucked in a breath when she heard that. The vampiress had told them she hadn't known the victim. Somehow the admission didn't surprise Lyra. The woman was involved in this. She was too arrogant in her vampirism not to be. She was one of those who considered herself better than all the races in the world.

Hand on the knob, Caine turned back to Kellen. "For what it's worth, Kellen, I'm sorry."

The vampire waved Caine's condolences away with a brisk flick of his hand. "No worries, Chief. I'll be out of your hair before I go completely insane. I see an extended vacation in my future."

Caine left Kellen in the room while the team reassembled in the nearby conference area. Everyone looked grim and unsettled.

Lyra, Jace and Eve took seats at the table, while Caine stood at the head. Dark circles rimmed his eyes and his face was paler than usual.

"Looks like Kellen may have given us our first solid suspect in this case," Caine said.

"Nadja Devanshi," Lyra said.

Caine nodded. "I have a call in to Mahina to bring her in."

"The baron isn't going to like that," Jace said.

"No, he's not, but I don't really care." Caine slumped into the chair behind him. "I'm tired of chasing our tails on this case. We've lost too much and I'm not willing to lose anything more."

Before anyone could respond, Caine's cell phone shrilled. He flipped it open. "Valorian."

Watching his face, Lyra knew in seconds that they'd run into another snag. Nothing had been easy on this case. Not with the first murders, not in San Antonio, and especially not now. It was all coming to a head. Lyra could feel it all the way down to her bones.

He snapped the phone shut and sighed. Looking around the table, he met everyone's gaze then locked onto Lyra. Her heart lurched into her throat.

"We have another DB."

Chapter 18

Lyra's stomach lurched into her throat as Caine pulled onto the curb behind Mahina's unmarked sedan in front of New Destiny. While the others jumped out of the SUV, she stayed behind. She felt cold inside. Her limbs were freezing from the inside out and she couldn't move from her seat. It was as if *she* had rigor mortis.

Caine opened her door. "Do you want to stay in the vehicle?"

She shook her head, hating being coddled. She'd been doing this job long enough to see all manner of death and destruction. Another body, whoever it may be, was just another case. She had to remember that.

Even if she had just seen the victim only hours before.

Taking in a deep breath, Lyra slid out of the vehicle, went around back and grabbed her kit. She followed

Caine and Eve into the shop. The officer stationed at the doorway nodded to them as they passed.

Inside, it looked the same way it had when she'd left it earlier. There didn't seem to be anything broken. No blatant evidence that a fight had taken place. The only difference was the smell that permeated the store, overcoming the patchouli.

The scent of death.

There was no other odor as pungent.

"It's a mess," the police captain said, licking her lips. "I haven't come across a scene like this in years."

"Who called it in?" Caine asked.

"Anonymous tip."

"Hmm, I'm thinking not so anonymous," Caine said as he peered through the hanging strings of beads. "Too convenient."

Mahina grunted in agreement as Caine swept the curtain aside and stepped into the back office. Eve followed him through, Lyra the last in line, snapping on latex gloves.

She tried to avert her eyes, forcing them to the floor to look for evidence, but no matter what she did, Lyra couldn't help but stare at the witch sitting in the chair she'd been in only hours before. Lyra had to put a hand to her mouth to stop the gasp of revulsion.

Black candles stuck out from where Claire's eyes should have been. The wicks had been lit and still flickered with tiny flames. Blood and entrails pooled beneath the table and chair. The poor woman had been gutted.

After the crime-scene photos were taken, Caine and the medical examiner sat the body up so he could take a body-temperature reading to determine time of death.

Sliding the thermometer in, Givon read the gauge. "According to liver temp, she's been dead from four to eight hours." He took it out and gestured to the victim's stiffening arms. "Rigor is setting in."

"I was here maybe three hours ago," Lyra interjected.

Givon frowned. "Are you positive?"

Lyra nodded.

"Then, I'm leaning more toward the three as livor mortis is almost fixed along her legs and buttocks where she's been sitting."

Caine locked eyes with Lyra. He knew she had been here following a lead, but she hadn't had the chance to tell him what she had learned from Claire. Despite the lapse, Lyra knew exactly what Caine was thinking. This was another warning—to her.

She heard it loud and clear.

The witch had died horribly because the killer thought she had told Lyra something. It made her sick to her stomach.

The woman had died for no reason.

As she followed Caine's orders and snapped pictures of the various objects around Claire's office, nothing seemed out of place. The drawers of her desk were closed. Testing the middle, she found it locked. It didn't appear as if the killer had been looking for anything.

Except for what he achieved in the witch's murder.

"What exactly did the victim tell you, Lyra?" Caine asked, as he examined the wound in the body's abdomen.

"She established that this was probably the last place Lori James was before she died. And that Lori bought some items that could be used in demon summoning, before leaving in a dark-colored sedan. Someone else had been driving."

Caine nodded. "That establishes a time line and that Lori could be involved in the other demon-summoning ceremonies."

"That definitely casts more suspicion on Nadja Devanshi," Eve added. "She lied about knowing Lori and she owns a black Mercedes."

"Yeah, but we're still missing something," Caine said as he looked up from inspecting the body. "It doesn't all add up."

Lyra continued to search around the room, her eyes on the floor. That was when she spied the corner of a white paper peeking out from under the desk. Crouching down, she slowly dragged it out with the tip of her gloved finger.

Her name was scrawled across the small envelope in black ink.

Glancing behind her, she made sure that both Caine and Eve were looking elsewhere as she scooped up the envelope and opened it. Inside was a message to her, scrawled in shaky handwriting. *Lyra, it comes for you on your day.*

"Lyra, did you find something?" Caine asked.

Standing, she showed him the note.

Without comment, he glanced at it then nodded. "Bag it and tag it." Then went back to work.

For another hour, the three of them processed the scene, staying until the medical examiner's office bagged the body and put it into the ambulance to be taken to Givon's freshly cleaned office back at the lab. So far, since the morgue hadn't been damaged, he'd been the only one able to get back into his old digs. The other areas were still being picked over and cleaned.

Stripping off her gloves, Lyra moved into the shop

away from the others. She needed privacy to register the warning in the note. Maybe it had nothing to do with this case and everything to do with this nagging feeling that something was up with Theron.

After stripping off his gloves and shoving them into his crime-scene vest pocket, Caine walked over to her. She could see on his face that what he was going to say to her, she wasn't going to like one bit.

"I can't let you leave here on your own, Lyra. I'm assigning you a bodyguard."

"Don't you think you're being irrational?"

Caine eyed her. "You think I'm being irrational? Who's calling the kettle black here?"

She swallowed, knowing full well what he was referring to. The evidence bag in her kit ticked like a time bomb. "I can certainly see the point of police protection, but a bodyguard? I don't need someone following me around all the time."

"Yes, you do," he said firmly. "Don't you get it? The killer didn't come here because the victim knew too much. The killer came here because he was following you."

"You don't know that for sure."

"Don't I?" He arched that damn brow of his again. She hated that smug look of his, as if he knew everything. The fact that he had acute powers of reason and deduction didn't matter to her. He had to be wrong. Had to. She couldn't live with herself knowing that she brought this death upon Claire.

"What's wrong with the police presence at my house?"

"It's not enough." He gestured to the back room from where two techs were carrying out the body. "I think this attests to that fact."

She opened her mouth to protest again, when another voice sounded behind her.

"I'll do it."

Lyra swung around to see Theron standing behind her, his face stoic and unreadable.

"The hell you will," she stammered.

He promptly ignored her and spoke to Caine. "I'll stay with her. It makes sense anyway since we still have work to do on the book."

Frowning, Caine eyed him. "I'm trusting you with her life, Theron. Are you sure you're up to the task?"

"She'll be safe with me. I can guarantee you that."

Caine nodded, then proceeded to leave the shop with Eve in tow.

"Hey, did anyone ask me?" Lyra demanded.

Theron faced her and frowned. She'd never seen him look so angry before. It was not a look she enjoyed seeing. "Stop being foolish, Lyra. My presence may save your life." Lifting his chin, he turned toward the door. "I'll be waiting outside for you. We can have a proper dinner this time at your home."

Shocked, Lyra watched him open the door and step outside. Her shock soon turned to anger. Pushing up her sleeves, she gripped her kit tight and moved to the door. Fury simmered at the surface of her skin. Fear did that to her.

"Yeah, but who's going to save yours?" she mumbled.

Chapter 19

Nerves humming, Lyra unlocked the front door of her house and let Theron inside. She'd had only two other men in her house—her last boyfriend, after three months of dating, and Caine. And she'd never let either one of them near her bedroom. Not that she was thinking about letting Theron in that room, either.

She watched in anticipation as he surveyed the living room, his hands clasped together. Why his opinion mattered was beyond her, but it did. She didn't want him to think her uptight or anal retentive because everything in her place was neat, tidy and organized. She liked order and couldn't stand it when everything was in disarray. It threw her off balance. She couldn't think when she was like that.

Like the way Theron was making her feel right now, touching her things.

He turned from inspecting a vivid watercolor of Lyra among a field of flowers. "Pretty." He smiled. "It suits you."

The compliment warmed her cheeks and other parts of her anatomy. "My grandmother painted it."

"Eleanore had many talents."

"Did you know my gran?" she asked, her interest piqued by the way he had arched a brow at her name.

He shook his head. "Not personally. I was barely coming into my own magic when I heard she had died. I was a late bloomer. But my mother talked of her fondly. Her greatness was well known, even across the ocean."

"Yes, she was a great woman," Lyra agreed.

Still am.

Lyra smiled at her gran's comment.

Tilting his head, Theron regarded her intently. What was he looking for? she wondered. What did he see?

Clearing her throat, she gestured to the kitchen. "Can I get you something to drink?"

"Wine, if you have it."

"I'm sorry, I don't. I don't normally drink."

"Tea, then."

In the kitchen, she filled the teakettle and put it on the stove. Taking out two cups, she dropped tea bags inside them and waited for the water to boil.

Having Theron in her house was going to take some getting used to. She could hear him pacing her living room, inspecting the various items on her shelves and tables. And she could smell his intoxicating scent—a mix of exotic spices and the outdoors. All witches had an earthy odor to them, but because of Theron's vampiric genetics, his smell was more potent. Sexual in nature.

Lyra couldn't help but take another deep breath. She closed her eyes as his delicious scent wrapped around her, coiling over her skin, permeating her pores. Sweet, rich and addictive. Would she ever get the fragrance out of her mind? She swayed as the kettle whistled. Her eyes snapped open and she shook her head to clear it. He shouldn't be here. This close. It was too dangerous. Theron made her want things, sinfully delicious things.

She poured the boiling water into the cups over the tea bags, stirring each three times before pulling the bags out. Lyra carried them into the living room where Theron had finally settled onto the sofa.

Handing him the cup, she said, "I hope chamomile is okay."

"It's perfect, thank you." He took a sip then set his cup down on the coaster on the coffee table.

As Lyra sipped the hot, soothing liquid, she watched Theron over the rim. After what they'd already been through, drinking tea together seemed like such a ridiculously simple thing to engage in.

Simple and Theron did not go together.

Nothing had been simple since seeing him again. Not her job, not the case, not even her feelings. She'd been muddled since Nouveau-Monde, and she couldn't seem to shake that strange sensation. No matter what she did. Having him in her home didn't help matters, but she didn't think that was going to change soon. She never saw him look so determined. She had a feeling the only way she'd be able to get away from him was with a complicated binding spell and an invisibility charm.

He smiled at her again, humor lighting up his face. "You have the most expressive eyes, Lyra, of any woman I've met."

Blushing, she lowered her gaze onto the errant thread on her pants and tugged at it.

"You're not going to be able to get rid of me so easily with one of your binding spells."

"Am I that transparent?"

"Sometimes."

"I don't like to be boxed in and told what to do. It feels like a—"

"Cage," he finished for her.

She nodded.

He reached for her hand and stilled her fidgeting. "I know how you feel, Lyra. Try living under a domineering vampire father."

She met his gaze and saw a flash of regret and pain cross his face. She hadn't realized what his childhood must have been like with a powerful vampire for a father and a witch for a mother. It was no wonder that Theron had come off so haughty and refined when she had first met him. He had likely been raised to believe that his vampire side was better than his witch half. She imagined that his father probably taught him to loathe his witch side. She couldn't imagine not liking a part of herself, especially such an important and powerful part.

"Your father raised you?" she asked.

He nodded. "Vampire children are hard to come by, so he made it his priority to raise me as one."

"What about your mother?"

"Cecelia tried her best to exert some influence on me, but Lucien, he is not a man who allows anyone else to have power, especially over him." He smiled without humor, picking up his tea and taking a sip. "Once I turned eighteen, I sought my mother out and began my magical training in secret."

"Did he ever find out?"

"Oh, yes, but once he discovered how powerful I had become and the uses for my magic, he had no problem with it at all."

Lyra could hear the derision in his voice and decided not to press him any further. It was obvious that he harbored some animosity toward his father, and rightly so.

"I think my stomach is growling. How 'bout we eat?" Lyra said, changing the subject. After setting her cup on the table, she jumped up and marched into the kitchen.

"Yes, I am a bit hungry, as well," Theron said.

Lyra opened her refrigerator, just now remembering she didn't have any food.

Why did it feel so hot in here all of a sudden? Lyra's palms were sweating and she wanted to wipe her mouth where she was sure there was sweat beading on her top lip. She was hungry, too, but maybe, like Theron, for more than just food.

"Ah, I forgot that I haven't been shopping since returning from France, so there's nothing in the fridge to cook." She moved past him to grab the phone. "How about takeout? Do you like Thai?"

He reached for the refrigerator and opened the door. "You'd be surprised what kind of delicious meal I can create out of virtually nothing."

"I'll just order in, Theron. You don't need to cook."

"I want to," he said as he plunked a bag of celery and a half jar of tomato sauce onto the counter. "It relaxes me."

Amused, and a little bit touched, she watched as he rummaged through her cupboards then came away with a box of macaroni and cheese. He took out the cheese pack and set the box of noodles next to the pot he found in one of the other cupboards.

When he swung around to look at her, she put her hand to her mouth to hide the smile blossoming on her face. His eyes were dancing, and the corners of his beautiful mouth twitched.

"You must have a garden, Lyra. No upstanding witch is without one."

"Yes, I have one."

"Good. You are in charge of collecting whatever is ripe. We can't have this delicious pasta—" he picked up the box of macaroni "—without our vegetables, now can we?"

"No, we certainly can't."

Laughing and feeling lighter than she had in more months than she could count, Lyra slid open the balcony door and wandered down to her small greenhouse. A man she was starting to really like was making her dinner. She found the situation surreal, but it didn't stop the warm sensation from growing in her heart.

Chapter 20

While they cooked dinner together, Theron couldn't take his eyes off Lyra. After returning from the garden with red peppers, carrots and snow peas, she chopped them up and sautéed them in a light olive oil. She had this very subtle feminine way of moving that made his heart pick up a beat and his groin twitch to the rhythm.

Oblivious to her own womanly power, Lyra was the most sensual being he'd ever encountered.

They made small talk as they put the simple dish together, comparing herbs they used and foods they utilized to make healing tinctures and potions. For the first time since arriving in Necropolis, Theron felt comfortable and relaxed. Unguarded. There was no ulterior motive to his actions as he boiled pasta and added spices to the tomato sauce. Usually, if he made dinner for a woman, it was to seduce and entice—the ultimate goal of ending in bed together for a night of unbridled passion. But not this time, not with Lyra. His only motive was to feed her empty stomach and ease the troubled thoughts he knew she harbored.

The case was taking its toll on her. He could see it in her eyes. She was afraid. And he didn't think that was a common emotion for the little spitfire witch.

They ate by candlelight at the small dining table. He knew Lyra didn't light the jasmine-scented candles with any motive other than to perfume the air with a pleasing and relaxing aroma. Yet he found the gesture very romantic.

Having taken her last bite of food, Lyra set her fork down on the table and leaned back in her chair. "That was so good."

"You sound surprised."

"I am." She chuckled. "Even though you do come across as a man of many talents." She rose and grabbed her plate to take to the kitchen.

From another woman, he would've taken that as a compliment or as an innuendo about his bedroom talents, but from Lyra it sounded full of amusement. Theron stood, taking the plate from her hand.

She held firm. "I'll take it. It's no problem."

"Lyra, let me do this small thing."

Maybe she finally sensed his eagerness to please her in some way because she let go of the plate and nodded. "Okay."

"Go and sit," he suggested as he moved into the kitchen and set the dirty dishes by the sink. "Would you like more tea?"

"No, thanks."

Theron returned to the living room, where Lyra was

sitting on the sofa, his big book open on her lap. Her lips moved as she read the text, her index finger tracing the lines. He watched her mouth, remembering the kiss they'd shared. It had literally been electric. Still the sensation of her magic rolled over his skin like a current. He wondered if it would ever dissipate, even after he went back to France, back to his life. Did he even want it to?

Taking the opportunity of her distraction, he settled on the cushions next to her. Careful not to bump her leg, he still sat close enough so he could inhale the stimulating scent of her floral perfume.

"There's this one part that's really bugging me. I look at it and think I should know what it means, but I can't seem to reason it out."

Theron glanced down at the passage and symbols she was referring to. It was the part that he had already figured out, or thought he had. He knew she would figure it out eventually. She was a smart lady, but for now, he didn't want her to worry, to fear. If he could keep that from her, he would.

Sliding his hands under the book, he picked it up and snapped it closed. She flinched at the action.

"No work right now." He set the book onto the table.

"Theron, it's important for us to figure that out."

"I know." He turned so he was facing her. "Just give us another half hour to relax before we have to deal with the case again. A half hour, that's all I ask."

She eyed him and he could see the wheels whirling in her mind, trying to decide what he was up to, and whether she liked it.

"Okay." Her gaze was scrutinizing, weary even, as she searched for his angle. He smiled because of it.

Her blatant innocence turned him on, like nothing

before. She was more enthralling than any scantily clad woman with a come-hither look.

"Could you hold me for a while?" She rubbed her hands on her arms. "I haven't been able to shake this cold creeping over me since seeing Claire's body."

Nodding, he gathered her in his arms, too over-whelmed for words. Fear pinched her features. It made his stomach clench and his heart ache. Two sensations he wasn't familiar with under these circumstances, having never experienced them when it came to women.

She shivered in his arms, and he pressed her closer, wanting desperately to ease her shakes. Lifting a hand, he stroked her hair, letting the silky strands brush through his fingers. Cuddled close, Theron realized that she was really quite small, his *petite sorcière,* although she never came across that way. She had always seemed taller and stronger, until now. He was besieged with emotion that she chose to lift the veil in front of him. That she trusted him enough to allow him in.

He kissed the top of her head. "You're safe with me, Lyra. I promise I won't let anything happen to you."

Shifting her position, she looked at him. Her eyes were wet with tears. "I know you won't."

He could see the trust in her eyes and it nearly did him in.

Leaning down, he neared her lips inch by inch, afraid to go too fast, yet vibrating with a need to go faster. Her eyelashes fluttered as he stopped a mere whisper away. Her quickening breath puffed against his lips, warming them. He could smell chamomile and the spicy sauce they had just consumed. The urge to kiss her vibrated through his whole body, but he wanted her to breach the last inch between them. It had to be her choice.

"Kiss me, Theron," she breathed, quaking in his arms.

"No," he panted against her lips. "Kiss me."

Closing her eyes, she covered his mouth with hers and kissed him just as he asked. It was well worth the agony of waiting.

Cupping her cheeks, he tilted her head to deepen the kiss. She moaned into his mouth and he swallowed it down, eager for more, eager for whatever she'd give him. He was ravenous for her and hoped she didn't ask him to stop, because he wasn't sure if he could and still stay sane.

Careful not to scare her, Theron lowered his hands to her neck, caressing her, then down to her shoulders. She leaned into him as he moved his hands over her back. Lyra was receptive to his touch, urging him to be bolder.

Dragging his lips from her mouth, he pressed kisses to her chin, along her jawline and to her ear. He licked the outer edge of her lobe, then sucked the sensitive flesh into his mouth.

Fisting her hands into his shirt, she pulled on him, bringing him closer as he nibbled on her ear. Every stroke of his tongue brought heated gasps of pleasure from her lips. He loved the little sounds she made. He wanted to hear more. By the end, he needed her to be screaming his name.

"Ton beauté m'écrase," he panted.

"What does that mean?" she breathed, her voice catching with the things he was doing at her neck.

"Your beauty crushes me."

Sighing, she ran her hands through his hair. "By the moon, I love French."

Chuckling, he continued to lick and suckle the flesh

on her neck just under her ear. He moaned just thinking about how responsive she'd be when he touched her between the thighs. He knew she'd be hot and wet for him.

Slowly, Theron moved his hand over and cupped her breast. He was rewarded with a low mew and gasp of delight. She matched the size of his palm, and he could feel her rigid nipple through the thin cotton of her shirt. He closed his eyes and nearly sobbed, knowing that she'd fit perfectly into his mouth.

Caressing her, he rubbed his thumb over her taut peak, glorying in the sudden pants she gave. He couldn't wait to have her naked and beneath him. He wanted to watch her face as he eased into her inch by inch, knowing that he'd be her first. Knowing that he would be giving her that pleasure. Him and only him.

With deft fingers, Theron began to unbutton her shirt. After the fourth one, he slid his hand inside and cupped her breast again. The simple cotton of her bra made him groan. He never knew ordinary cotton could drive him mad with desire. But it did. He needed to see her in it, all of her.

Tugging at the shirt, he pulled it up and finished undoing the last button. Theron pushed the two sides apart and looked his fill of her. He bit down on his lip to stop the groan. Her creamy skin glowed against the simple light blue color of her bra. He had the desperate urge to trail his tongue along the curves of her breasts heaving above the cotton.

"So beautiful, my *petite sorcière*."

"I'm not."

He could see her struggling to cover herself with her hands.

"You are more beautiful to me than any woman. I wish you could see yourself as I do."

"Theron—"

He pressed a finger to her lips. He didn't want to hear her uncertainty. If it was the last thing he ever did, he would make her see just how extraordinary she truly was.

"No, tonight I will show you your beauty." Leaning down, he pressed his lips to hers and kissed her again, eagerly, thoroughly, so she would know just how much he desired her.

Twining her fingers into his hair, she held on as he trailed moist kisses along her chin, down her neck and to her chest. She took in short ragged breaths as he lowered his mouth to the swell of her breasts. He pressed his lips to the top of one breast then the other, inhaling her mouthwatering scent each time. His head was dizzy from her, intoxicated, drunk on her smell and the taste of her skin.

With one finger, he pulled on the cup of her bra to reveal one perfect nipple, tight and flushed. Eager to taste her skin, he bent down to press his mouth to her flesh.

The shrill of a cell phone startled him and he halted before he could touch her.

Clearly flustered, Lyra turned and made a grab for the phone that sat on the table. Theron held her around the waist but that didn't stop her from nearly falling off the sofa in the process. She managed to snatch the cell before she landed face-first onto the carpet.

She flipped it open. "It's Lyra." She avoided his gaze as she murmured into the phone. By the short clipped answers, Theron knew it was Caine calling.

Shutting the phone, she set it on the table then pulled her shirt closed. It was a surefire end to the evening. She didn't have to say a word. He could read it in her eyes. Her guard came up instantaneously. It was a marvel to behold.

She was no longer the pliant, vulnerable woman that he had shared dinner with but the no-nonsense crime-scene investigator back at her job.

"That was Caine," she said as she buttoned her shirt quickly. "Nadja's agreed to come in. Mahina's going to do the interview right away."

"You don't have to be there, do you?"

"No, but I want to be."

Theron released his hold on her and pushed back on the sofa, putting physical distance between them to mimic the palpable distance already solidifying.

"Well, then I guess we should get to the station." He stood and straightened his shirt, noticing that his pants were going to be a lot harder to straighten. He ached like a sonofabitch.

"I'm sorry, Theron," she said, gazing at him with something akin to sympathy in her eyes.

He shook his head and waved away her apology. "I'll survive." He glanced down at the tent he made in his trousers and smiled. "Maybe."

Her lips lifted into a smile, and then they laughed together.

Chapter 21

Because of the damage to the underground parking, Lyra had to park her car outside the Necropolis Police Department in the visitor lot. A throng of reporters were milling about outside the main doors, and when she and Theron approached they perked up, pressed on fake smiles and thrust their microphones into Lyra's face.

"Ms. Magice, are the rumors true that Nadja Devanshi is involved in a series of grisly murders throughout Necropolis and the surrounding area?" The question came from Roxanne Parker, an unscrupulous lycan journalist from the *Necropolis Times*.

Ignoring her, Lyra tried to push past the reporter. Roxanne put her arm on Lyra to stop her from moving ahead. "Is it true that one of the murder victims looks exactly like you? Do you feel as if this is a direct threat to your safety?"

"No. Comment."

Theron, who had been behind Lyra, pushed ahead and grabbed the reporter's arm. "I suggest you remove your hand if you want to keep it intact."

Startled by the cutting comment, the lycan snatched her hand back and stared at Theron wide-eyed. A low growl sounded in the woman's throat, but that didn't deter the dhampir. In fact, he looked quite amused at her behavior. The dramatic arch of his brow and the rather bored expression on his face spoke volumes.

Wrapping his arm around Lyra's shoulder, Theron escorted her the rest of the way into the police station. After his remark, a path had been efficiently cut into the mob of reporters and the pair weren't bothered again.

As they walked through the lobby and to the back offices, Eve caught them on the fly. "Oh, you're here. Good." She ushered them quickly down the hallway. "Caine should've warned you about the press."

"Yeah, it's a circus out there."

"It's a circus in here, too," Eve added.

Stopping at a door near one of the interview rooms, Eve opened it and went in. Lyra and Theron followed her through. Caine, Jace and Tala were already inside, standing by the two-way mirror, watching the goings-on inside the interview room.

Jace glanced over his shoulder. "Welcome to the main attraction."

Without comment, Lyra took a position at the window. Inside, Mahina was standing behind the table, her back to them. On the other side of the table sat Nadja Devanshi and her lawyer, Robert, another vampire by the looks of his haughty facade and crisply pressed suit.

Nadja appeared calm and unaffected in her impeccable cream-and-navy dress. She fingered the strings of pearls at her neck while eyeing Mahina. Maybe the vampiress wasn't as impenetrable as she came across.

If anyone could break her, it would be the lycan police captain.

The lawyer began. "For the record, I'd like to remind you and the several people standing behind the mirror that Ms. Devanshi has voluntarily agreed to this interview. She wants the police to find the killer and put him away for life, as do we all."

"Noted," Mahina said. "Why did you lie to chief investigator Caine Valorian about knowing Lori James?"

"I wasn't aware that I had." Her voice was cool and aloof, like brittle ice. It sent a shiver down Lyra's spine.

"Two days ago at the club, he asked you if you knew Lori James, a witch who worked at the spa. You told him you didn't know her."

"If I told him that, then it must be true."

"We have a viable witness who claims that you knew the deceased very well. That you fed from her often enough to be more than casual acquaintances."

The lawyer cleared his throat. "If you're referring to one Kellen Falcon, the ballistics expert for the OCU, for one, he is a biased witness, as he works with Mr. Valorian. Two, he has recently been diagnosed with SC." He steepled his fingers on the table. "Not a very good witness in my opinion. A vampire slowly going mad. What else do you have because so far this is looking pretty pathetic and like a complete waste of time."

Nadja put her hand on his arm. "Come now, Robert, let them have their fun. It's obvious they have nothing better to do than to harass me. Look at the bright side. I've gotten a hell of a lot of publicity from this. It might help sell my new CD."

"Oh, she's a cold one," Jace commented.

"She's a bitch," Eve bit out.

Caine put his arm around her and squeezed her close. Lyra knew that Eve had had an encounter, brief but potentially hazardous, with the chanteuse during their earlier case.

Mahina appeared unaffected, but Lyra knew that underneath that facade, the police captain was likely fuming like a mad dog. "How is it that you know about Kellen's sickness when the lab just found out about it?"

"Oh, we've known at the club for some time that poor Kellen was suffering. The way he went through blood...we knew there had to be something wrong with him." Nadja twirled the pearls around her finger.

"I'm sure I can find someone else at the club to corroborate Kellen's claim," Mahina said.

Robert smiled. "Are you so sure about that, Captain Garner? My client is a founding member of the club and a regular contributor to its charity fund. I don't think you'll find anyone to say anything."

"This isn't going as I hoped," Lyra said.

Caine shook his head. "I know."

"And to think you listen to her music, Chief," Jace said.

"Not anymore, he doesn't," Eve announced. "I tossed her CDs eight months ago."

Mahina tried another angle. "You drive a black Mercedes with burgundy interior, don't you?"

"As do a lot of other people, Captain," Robert said, his frustration starting to show by the beads of sweat on his brow.

Mahina picked up a paper from the table. "Actually, only fifteen other people in Necropolis have cars with that exact make, model and interior color."

Robert chuckled. "If that's all the police have to go on, I'm afraid this interview is over." He stood, gathering his papers and briefcase. He slid his business card across the table to Mahina. "If you have any further questions, Captain, be sure to call me. Under no circumstances shall you speak to my client again."

Mahina ignored the card and glared across the table at Nadja, who had yet to stand. "Where were you two nights ago between seven o'clock and midnight?"

"Why, at the club, of course."

"Is there anyone who can confirm that?"

"About five or six people." She arched a brow regally. "Would you like their names?"

"Yes, I would." Mahina slid a piece of paper and a pen across the table to her.

After quickly scrawling five names down on the paper, Nadja smoothed down her dress and stood. She smiled into the mirror. It seemed to Lyra that she was looking right at her. Lyra's heart began to pound so loudly that she was sure everyone in the room could hear it. She felt someone stir at her side. She glanced at Theron as he took her hand. She squeezed it.

"Thank you for the stimulating conversation." Nadja inclined her head. "I hope we all can do this again soon. Oh, and, Caine, I'll be sure to see you at the Mistress's Centennial."

Robert opened the door for her and she left, her chin lifted high. Her lawyer followed her out, a parting sneer directed Mahina's way before he closed the door behind him.

Mahina swung around to look into the window. She shrugged. "That didn't go very well."

Caine pressed the button on the wall and spoke. "Meet us in the conference room. We'll go over what we have, what we don't, and what we just lost."

With a brisk nod of her head, Mahina marched out of the interview room, purposely leaving Nadja's lawyer's card on the table. Lyra knew the lycan did it as a snub. Mahina was one woman a person didn't want to be on the wrong side of. She could be tenacious as a rabid dog.

"Okay." Caine looked at the team. "As I was saying, let's reassemble in the conference room and get a game plan going, because this is going downhill like a freight train without brakes."

Mahina met them at the open door. "I'm going to the club to check out her alibi. I'll meet up with you later."

Caine nodded.

After filing out of the room, they walked down the hallway toward the conference room. The path led them by the lobby and as they neared, Lyra saw Nadja and her lawyer standing by the front desk chatting with two other people.

The baron was in midsentence. Lyra sucked in a breath at the sight of the other woman standing with them. She was more formidable in person than Lyra ever imagined. The other woman, a golden vampiress with ink-black hair and mesmerizing eyes, stood beside Laal, but her head turned their way as they neared.

The mistress of the city, Ankara Jannali, smiled, and Lyra was too stunned to do anything but stare at the striking woman as she neared. Most vampires were beautiful, but the mistress transcended mere beauty;

hers rose to an entirely new level. That was one of the
many reasons she was on the governing body of the city.
Almost too arresting to look at, Lyra had the urge to
shield her eyes.

"Lady Ankara." Caine bowed his head. "How may I
be of service?"

She glanced briefly at each of them, then her gaze
settled on Eve. Lyra could see Eve cringe away from the
mistress's intense gaze.

"This is your wife?"

Caine put his arm around Eve. It was both an act of
comfort and protection. "Yes. This is Eve."

Ankara's gaze flitted away from Eve and landed on
Lyra. The amulet at her throat nearly scalded her skin.
Reaching up, Lyra covered it with her hand, biting back
the urge to cry out from the searing pain.

Ego vocare
et animas
in fidem recipere
pax ex nox
omni malum APAGE TE!

Her grandmother's voice sounded all around her,
although Lyra knew she was the only one to hear it. Lyra
could feel the power of Eleanore's protection spell and
thanked the moon she had the presence of mind to cast
one, because Lyra had nearly been dumbstruck and
immobile by the vampiress's power.

Chapter 22

A small smile twitched at the mistress's mouth and she glanced at the ceiling. It was brief but Lyra had caught it. Had she somehow heard Eleanore's chant?

Mistress Jannali's attention turned to Theron and she smiled. "Ah, Theron LeNoir. I heard you were in my city. It surprises me that you have not come to see me. Your father would certainly disapprove of your lack of respect."

He bowed his head. "Lady Ankara, I meant no disrespect, but I have been engaged in helping the OCU with this abhorrent case. Finding the killer, I would think, is an important matter, and one I am sure you completely support as the mistress of the city."

Lyra risked a peek at Theron's face. He was looking directly at the mistress, unflinching. He was obviously a lot more powerful than she first thought, or that he had let on. Only the most powerful vampires could withstand looking directly at Mistress Jannali. Even Caine had a somewhat difficult time.

The mistress bristled slightly at his bold statement, then it passed and she was her usual, icy, fearsome self. Lifting her chin, she said, "Yes, these murders have become quite bothersome. The media is having a field day over it, but I have the utmost confidence that this lab will solve the case once you are on the right path."

With a flick of her hand, she gestured to Nadja Devanshi and her lawyer, still standing in the lobby watching the debacle unfolding. Lyra could sense a rise in Caine's power. It was obvious he wasn't happy with the innuendo the mistress was making.

"It is within our legal right to have questioned Ms. Devanshi concerning the murder of Lori James. She knew the victim and had the means."

Mistress Jannali waved her hand again. "Nonsense. Nadja is an upstanding citizen of Necropolis, and one of my most loyal campaign contributors. I've known her for a long time. That alone should be enough to dismiss the line of investigation that you seem so intent on pursuing."

"I'm within my right—"

She put her hand up to stop the next words. "There's nothing else that needs to be said, Caine. It's done. And I'd better not hear that Nadja has been further inconvenienced or harassed." Arching a brow and smiling, she regarded them and continued, having thoroughly dismissed Caine's argument. "Now, I hope to see you all at my centennial celebration." She moved closer to Theron and said, "And you, Monsieur LeNoir, we will have our time together soon. I'll send a car for you. You're staying at the Saint Mark, are you not?"

A knot of jealousy twisted in Lyra's stomach as she

watched Lady Ankara gobble up Theron with her eyes. It was blatant and the mistress knew it, reveled in it even.

"Yes," he answered.

"I'll see you tomorrow, then, for tea."

He inclined his head. "I'm looking forward to it."

After a regal nod of her chin, the mistress turned and floated back down the hall to where Nadja and her lawyer were still waiting. Once she moved to them, they all left the station house together.

Without a word, Caine walked down the hall toward the conference room, his arm still around Eve. Jace and Tala followed. Theron moved to go next, but Lyra stopped him with a steely gaze and a hand on her hip.

"You're not going to have tea with that woman, are you?"

"I don't really have a choice, Lyra. She is the mistress of the city and I'm a visitor. Etiquette dictates that at some point I do have to pay my respects to her."

"Vampire politics sucks."

Grinning, he stroked her hair. "I know. But this is something I have to deal with because of the LeNoir name."

She warmed inside from the subtle contact he made with her.

"You should change your name," she mumbled.

"If only it were that easy."

Swinging his arm around her, he steered her down the hall. They walked together to the conference room. Everyone else was sitting by the time the two of them strolled in. More than one set of eyebrows lifted when they arrived.

Avoiding the penetrating gazes, Lyra slid into a chair. Theron took the one next to her.

"You're pretty chummy with the mistress," Jace grunted at Theron.

"I have the distinct feeling that no one gets *chummy* with that woman."

Jace's lips twitched. He tried to hide it, but Lyra saw it before he could turn his head. It was obvious that Theron was starting to grow on him. The thought pleased Lyra. Like having a brother approve of your boyfriend.

Boyfriend? Lyra shook her head, trying to dislodge any notion of that occurring, and then forced her attention back to Caine.

"Obviously, the interview with Nadja didn't go as planned," Caine started. "And now the mistress has thoroughly ended our pursuit of that line of investigation."

"She was lying, Chief," Jace grunted. "However much I think Kellen is a lunatic, I believe him about what he saw."

Caine nodded. "I know. I do, too. But her lawyer was right. Kellen wouldn't make a very good witness. We need hard evidence against her if we want to pursue that path."

"What about the car?" Tala asked. "That's hard evidence."

"Yes, but there are fifteen other names on that list, as well. That alone is stopping a judge from granting us a warrant to search her vehicle. That and the mistress."

Eve picked up the vehicle list. "You know, the mistress's aide, Jerome Spindler, is on this list."

"Yes, that one has intrigued me the most," Caine said.

"You think she's involved with these murders?" Lyra asked.

Everyone at the table glanced at one another, sharing their fears and speculations. The answer was written on every face. Yes.

Lyra had her suspicions, as well. When her gran had spoken, she had the distinct impression that Lady Ankara had heard it, too. When she glanced up, the mistress had looked directly at where Eleanore had been hovering and smirked. Only those connected to the spirits, or those with one foot in and one foot out between the living and the dead, could actually see the lingerers.

"If the mistress is involved, then we are all in a lot of trouble," Jace said, stating the obvious. Mistress Jannali was the most powerful vampire in Necropolis, most likely in the world. If she were at the heart of this evil plan to open a gateway to hell, then they were royally screwed and might as well gather the marshmallow-roasting sticks and prepare for a rise in temperature.

Fire and brimstone were the least of their worries. If a portal was opened it would be the things that came through—demons in all their gruesome glory—that would be troublesome. More murder and mayhem would be at the top of their lists of things to do on a holiday in Necropolis.

"If we decide to follow through on this theory, we need to keep everything hush-hush. Everything. No one outside this room except for Mahina can know what we are planning or thinking."

Jace, Tala and Eve glanced at Theron. Lyra had the distinct urge to tell them to keep their comments to themselves. She could read what they were thinking on their faces. That he wasn't one of them.

Theron cleared his throat. "I realize that I am not part of this team and you have not known me long, but I have a way in that none of you seem to possess."

Caine arched his brow but the corners of his mouth lifted. Obviously he knew what Theron was insinuating.

"You're right. The mistress doesn't know you but she obviously thinks highly of your family name. That could go far, and to top it off, you've been invited to her home."

"Exactly what I was thinking." Theron smiled.

Lyra bolted forward in her seat. "You want Theron to spy on the mistress for us?"

"Yes," Caine said simply.

Except for Theron, everyone objected at once.

"Are you crazy?" Jace asked.

Eve set her hand on Caine's arm. "Are you sure that's the best option, considering what's been happening?"

"Theron is neither a detective nor a crime-scene investigator. He's an untrained civilian and you can't send him into a viper's nest with an agenda, Caine." Lyra clenched her hands. She couldn't believe they were even entertaining the thought. "The mistress has more power than all of us put together. She'll figure it out. And even if she isn't guilty of these crimes, she still has enough power to fire us all and make our lives miserable."

"That's all true, Lyra, but I think it's a risk we should take. I'm done following the rules. I want to end these murders and find whoever is responsible. I am willing to use whatever means are at my disposal. This is something no one will expect us to do."

Lyra glanced at Theron. He had yet to speak, but he

didn't need to. She could see his answer all over his face. He was determined to do this, no matter what the cost.

"You don't have to do this, Theron. It's not your responsibility."

He locked eyes with her, and she saw the dark presence there again in the molten lead depths. "I know. But if I have an opportunity to make a difference in this case, I'll take it."

Caine nodded. "Thank you, Theron."

"Buddy, it's your funeral," Jace added, shaking his head. "She's about the only vampire who scares the crap out of me."

Tala punched him in the arm. "I thought you weren't scared of anything, tough guy."

Jace grinned and tried to steal a kiss from his wife. "Just you, my love."

She swatted him away.

"The job comes with risks, which you should know about," Caine said. "Ankara is very powerful and very persuasive but most of her power lies in her touch. Try not to let her touch you. If she does, you will be more susceptible to her vampiric charms."

"I am half vampire. I am not without my defenses."

"Granted, but even I have fallen sway to her once or twice in the past."

Theron nodded. "I will keep that in mind."

"When it's over, I'll make sure you are well compensated."

"I'm not doing it for money. I have enough to last me a lifetime or two." He reached across the table and grasped Lyra's hand.

Tears nearly came to her eyes at the intensity of his

gaze. It was penetrating and she could feel it piercing her very heart. He was doing it for her. Maybe he felt more for her than she thought. Maybe there could be a future for them.

Her heart clenched at the thought, knowing it might not survive finding out the truth.

Chapter 23

The mistress's car arrived for Theron at half past two the next day, as promised.

He didn't know what he was expecting when he stepped from the hotel lobby outside to the waiting car, but it was not a Mercedes S-Class, the very car on the OCU's vehicle list.

The driver held the door for him while Theron slid into the backseat. Glancing around, he tried to take everything in—the condition of the seats, any stains on the floor carpet, any odd or out-of-place odors. On first inspection, everything appeared neat and tidy. What was he expecting to find? A note that said *I killed Lori James*.

As the car pulled away from his hotel, Theron considered that maybe he had committed himself to something he just wasn't cut out for. Lyra had been right; he was no detective or investigator. How could his inexperienced eye possibly find any evidence they needed for the case?

Maybe he wasn't up for this challenge. He had volunteered strictly out of his growing feelings for Lyra. He suffered a perpetual need to prove himself to her. Maybe to himself as a way to make amends for past transgressions. But he speculated that, at some point, that need just might get him killed in the process.

Twenty minutes later, the Mercedes stopped in front of a large iron gate. The driver used a remote and the gate slowly swung open, allowing them entrance. The driveway to the house was even longer than on his estate. He noticed other high-end vehicles lining the drive when they pulled up in front of a sprawling two-story mansion. Theron tried not to be impressed or intimidated. He had grown up wealthy and been surrounded by glitz and glamour his whole life. But just now he realized that Lady Ankara Jannali was wealthier than the LeNoirs, and far more powerful.

From this point, he'd been operating on the assumption that he had everything under control. He was a powerful man, with an arsenal of spells at his disposal, if needed. The absolute power radiating from the house forced him to grimace. He could sense negative energy skimming the surface of his skin, seemingly trying to wriggle its way in through his pores. Goose bumps rose on his arms and legs. This was an energy he'd never felt before and certainly had never dealt with. Just who was Lady Ankara Jannali?

When the driver opened the back door for him and escorted him to the front of the Jannalis' manor, Theron knew he had been fooling himself into thinking he had come prepared. It had all been an illusion. A witch's greatest trick.

The front door opened and a uniformed man ushered him in. "Right this way, Mr. LeNoir. The mistress has been expecting you."

Theron followed the butler through a grand foyer and to the left of a double-sided winding staircase to the second floor. He was led into a small and elegantly decorated room, adorned with priceless art. A small table in the center had already been set with cups and a teapot. Paintings—original Monets—hung on the walls and spectacularly crafted stone and bronze statues were displayed in various ways—on the floor and in glass display cases. It was obvious that the mistress shared his love of collecting. Meeting him in this room for their visit had been a wise strategy on her part.

He didn't wait long before Lady Ankara swept into the room, dressed in a floor-length gown of crimson. The color set off her dark skin and amber eyes magnificently. Theron had to suppress the urge to drink his fill of her. He couldn't deny that she was enthralling to look at, a lithe creature of extreme beauty and elegance. He could plainly see why she had become mistress of the city. The commanding glint in her eyes as she surveyed him, scrutinizing him from head to toe, her dominance and dominion over every situation.

"I am pleased you accepted my invitation, Theron." Once she spoke, she sat regally in one of the chairs.

Bowing his head, Theron waited until she was seated before he did. "It was an invitation I couldn't resist."

She picked up the teapot and poured tea into his cup then into her own. When she was done, he waited until she picked up her cup and took a sip. It was considered impolite to drink before the hostess, especially when she was more powerful.

"How is your father?" she asked after drinking and setting the cup down.

"Very well, thank you." Theron sipped from his cup. The lavender taste surprised him. It was an interesting choice for an afternoon tea. Had it been deliberate? Lavender was infamous for masking other tastes, especially ingredients used to invoke spells and herbal poisons like valerian root.

He set the cup down and dabbed at his mouth with his napkin, using it as a mask to actually spit the mouthful of tea into it. With his hand, he covered it and set it back into his lap. Hopefully, she didn't notice.

"It has been some years since I've seen Lucien." She smiled. "But my memories of him are quite fond."

"He will be overjoyed to hear that, Lady Ankara. I will be certain to tell him when I return to Nouveau-Monde."

"Are you planning to return soon?"

"When my work is done."

"Yes, I heard you were working with Caine and his team on these ghastly murders." She regarded him with a slight tilt of her head. "It's very noble of you."

Theron had the distinct feeling she was being sardonic in her retort. As if she knew he was nothing of the sort. Did she know about his past? He wondered how much of his father's business she was privy to. Had they been intimate to have shared such secrets?

"I'm doing what I can. If my knowledge of various *things* can help capture a killer, then I would certainly share that information."

"Hmm, interesting." She took another sip of her tea, then gestured to Theron's cup. "You don't like the tea?"

Theron smiled. "I'm afraid my stomach isn't agreeing with the flavor. So you will excuse me if I don't drink anymore."

"Of course." She returned his smile. But Theron didn't feel any warmth from it. "Do you like my collection?" She gestured to the various artifacts arrayed around the room.

"Yes, it's magnificent." He stood and inspected a particularly interesting bronze sculpture of a horned beast. "This looks Old Kingdom Egyptian."

She stood and joined him at the display case. "It is. You have a good eye."

"I have quite a few pieces from later eras, but nothing that early in history. I didn't even realize anything of this caliber had been unearthed. Where did you acquire it?"

"We all have our secrets." She stood close, her power pushing and pulling on him. She smiled again and this time shivers rushed down his spine. He suppressed the urge to recoil from her. She ran her finger over the glass. "This is mine. What's yours?"

Oh Lord, he wanted to recoil. Her presence was bearing down on him like a hundred-pound weight. He didn't know how much longer he could withstand it without having to drop to his knees to release the pressure on his body.

"If I tell you, it wouldn't be a secret, now would it?" he retorted, trying to play her game and keep her from seeing how much agony he was in.

By the glint in her eyes, she knew perfectly well how much he was suffering. She was a woman who didn't do anything without intent.

"It's okay, Theron. I already know your secret."

He felt like the room had closed in on him. His lungs

couldn't fill with air. He was being crushed from the inside out. Was she doing it? Or was it his own anxiety putting the clamp of fear on his body?

He reached out and placed his hand on the display case to keep from falling over. Sweat had beaded on his brow and lip. He felt a trickle run down his temple. She was grinning at him now, fully aware she had him by the balls.

"I know why you're here, Theron." Her voice came to him as a whisper. He wanted to swipe at the prickly sensation her words made over his ear. But he was immobile—as if frozen in place. Completely vulnerable to her.

"I came to pay my respects," he managed to say through the pressure in his head.

"You came to make sure I'll keep your secret. That I won't tell your friends in the OCU, especially the witch, about your naughty habits." She leaned into him, her mouth only inches from his. "Habits involving black magic," she purred.

"No," he spat, trying to shake his head.

Garbled whispers buzzed in his ears. He looked around the room, searching for the source.

"Oh, yes. I know what happened all those years ago, Theron. Your daddy told me all about it."

"I'm not that man anymore."

"Sure you are." She ran a finger over his mouth, down his neck and to his chest. She made a figure eight with her nail repeatedly on his shirt. "I can see the demon marks on you. I can see them when no one else can. Right there in your heart." She poked him hard in the chest.

Gritting his teeth, he tried to pull away from her. It

was futile; she was much too powerful. Again, the hushed murmurs sounded in his ears. Was there someone else in the room?

Trailing her finger back up, she rubbed it over his lips. "How did hurting that girl feel? Did you get off on it?" Her hand moved down again and cupped him through his pants. "Are you getting hard just thinking about it?"

"It was an accident."

"Of course it was, darling. Aren't they all just accidents? Your daddy cleaned it all up for you so no one would know. So no one would suspect that Theron LeNoir was a practitioner of the dark arts and a young innocent girl was hurt at his hands by his magic."

Tears rolled down Theron's cheeks. His negligence and ignorance of the black magic had cost a young girl her hands. They'd been burnt beyond repair. He had been young and foolish, thirsty for his own wealth and power. His quest had ended in tragedy. And, yes, he would do anything to keep that secret from the others, especially Lyra.

"Are you blackmailing me?"

She smiled again and chucked him under the chin. "My silence for yours."

"My silence in what? I don't know anything."

"Sure you do. Think back to your dark days, Theron, and it will come to you."

"I'm not that man anymore," he groaned, feeling like his larynx was being crushed in a steel vise.

"We'll soon see." The mistress patted him on the cheek and then gave him a quick kiss on the mouth.

Everything went black, as if the lights had been suddenly turned off in his mind. No sound or sensation could penetrate the dark surrounding him. He couldn't even feel himself. Where was he?

"You don't like the tea?"

The mistress's voice came through, startling Theron. Blinking back the moisture in his eyes, he gazed around, feeling disoriented and dizzy.

He was sitting at the table, a teacup in his hand, the taste of lavender on his lips.

Lady Ankara sat across from him, her cup sitting on the matching plate on the table. She was regarding him with curiosity.

Theron turned his head and looked around again. What had just happened? Had he imagined it all? Had it been a spell?

Feeling flushed, he set his cup down and picked up his napkin to dab at his mouth. The cloth of the napkin was unsoiled. "I'm afraid I'm not feeling well."

"Oh, I'm so sorry to hear that. Perhaps it would be best if my driver took you back to your hotel. Maybe you need to rest. I imagine working on this case has been very trying."

He nodded and stood, setting his napkin on the table. "It has, thank you."

"Well, I hope we can do this again soon, Theron."

"As do I, Lady Ankara." He bowed his head, sweat still dotting his upper lip.

"However brief, I did find our visit stimulating." She smiled.

His breath whooshed out of his lungs again. Without another word, Theron got up and left the house. The moment he was outside, he took in a few ragged breaths of cleansing air.

Although Theron didn't think he'd ever feel clean

again. Lady Ankara Jannali had effectively frightened him to the core. She had power he'd never even heard of someone possessing. And she knew his secret. That was a bad combination.

Chapter 24

The moment Theron returned to the lab and met with the team in the conference room, Lyra knew something had happened. His demeanor had changed and his eyes had a dark, haunted look. But he kept insisting that everything was fine when she asked him.

He kept his gaze fixed on the table as he spoke. "I didn't learn anything of importance. It was foolish to think I could."

"Did she say anything strange or out of context?" Caine asked. "You'd be surprised what has relevance or not."

"We drank tea and talked about my father and—" he paused, and Lyra saw uncertainty cross his face "—about collecting. She knew I was a collector and shared a favorite piece of hers."

"What piece?"

"An old Egyptian bronze statue. It had to have been over four thousand years old."

Caine frowned. "There has been a lot of speculation about Lady Ankara's origins. Maybe that statue has something to do with her heritage."

"Are you suggesting the mistress is a four-thousand-year-old Egyptian vampiress?" Jace asked.

"Yes, I am."

"But what has that got to do with our case?" Lyra asked.

"Probably nothing, but I find it interesting that she revealed that to Theron. The mistress doesn't do anything without purpose."

"Maybe she just likes Theron," Jace suggested, leaning forward on the table, clearly agitated. "He's an okay-looking guy, if you go for the European thing. Maybe she wants to date him."

Caine lifted a hand.

"Tell me everything that went on, Theron. Don't leave anything out. Something that may seem trivial to you could be just the link we are looking for."

"Her driver picked me up in a Mercedes—I'm assuming that's the vehicle that's on your list registered to him—and drove me to her home. I was escorted to her tearoom, which was also her collection room."

"What kind of collection?" Caine asked.

"Paintings, sculptures, ancient statues like the one I told you about…"

"Any books?"

Theron shook his head, then frowned. "Actually, yes, there were a few leather-bound tomes in the room, but they weren't under glass so I just assumed they were not part of her collection."

"What did she serve?" Caine asked.

"Tea."

"What kind?" Lyra could sense that Theron was holding something back. It was in the way he avoided Caine's gaze every time the chief asked a question. She had a feeling Caine could sense Theron's hesitancy, too.

Theron looked at her then. "Lavender."

"What? Why would she serve that?"

Caine leaned forward on the table. "I admit to never drinking any, but what's wrong with lavender tea?"

"It's not a usual blend and most times it is used for the sole purpose of masking something else in the tea, like a potion or a poison."

"Well, I think it's safe to say it wasn't poisoned, as Theron is still sitting here," Jace remarked.

Panic surging through her, Lyra set her hand on Theron's arm. "Were you spelled?"

"I don't know, maybe." He frowned. "I heard a lot of low whispering in the room, as if there had been several other people there."

"Were there?" Caine asked.

"Not that I could see."

"What else happened?" Lyra asked. "Did she do something to you?"

"No," he answered, as he pushed to his feet, effectively removing Lyra's hand from his arm. "And if you're through interrogating me, I think I will go out and get some air."

She watched as he left the conference room, concern filling her. It was obvious that something disturbing had happened to him at the mistress's and he was either too ashamed or too afraid to talk about it. A plethora of scenarios whizzed through Lyra's mind, all of them making her cringe with various emotions. Jealousy at the forefront. Had he succumbed to the mistress's seductive charms? Was that what he was hiding from her?

"The guy's hiding something," Jace grunted as he leaned back in his chair.

"We're treating him like a suspect, interrogating him," Eve said. "I'd be angry, too."

Caine nodded. "I agree, Eve. We asked him to do something, he did it, and we thanked him with an interrogation. He's a civilian, not a trained professional—we have to remember that."

Jace huffed. "I still think he's hiding something."

"Honey, you think everyone's hiding something." Tala patted Jace on the shoulder.

"Yeah, and I'm usually right." He turned his gaze to Lyra. "You need to be careful there, witchy."

"I don't know what you're talking about." Lyra sneered at him, feeling his gaze boring into her.

"Yes, you do."

Caine cleared his throat. "Okay, let's take a break, then reconvene in a couple of hours. We have the mistress's centennial to attend, but not until nine, so we have some time yet." He glanced down at the open folder on the table. "Jace, check in with Rick to see how he's doing with piecing Gwen's research back together. Eve, get with Givon and go over all the reports we have on our victims, past and present—make sure we're not missing anything. Tala, call Mahina and see where she's at with the other Mercedes owners. Someone driving one of those vehicles is involved somehow." He ran a hand through his hair. "Maybe they're all involved. We need to start putting some pressure on these people. Since Nadja's alibi held up, we need another prime suspect."

"You don't think the mistress is one?" Lyra asked.

"I don't know what to think at this point. We're losing this case. And the killer is winning. We can't let that happen."

Everyone got up and started filing out of the room to do their assigned tasks. Lyra was at the door when Caine called her back.

"Lyra, please stay for a minute."

Turning, she walked back to the table and sat in a chair near Caine. She felt the way she had when she was sent to the principal's office in high school for spelling the quarterback before the big football game.

"Is there something I should know about?"

She gnawed on her bottom lip. "Not that I can think of."

"About you and Theron?"

"I really hope you're not going to lecture me about getting involved with someone you work with, considering who you just recently married."

"No, I'm not going to lecture you." He eyed her intensely, and she could tell he was trying to wriggle his way into her emotions. "But I am going to tell you to be careful. Theron is a guarded man—that much is obvious. I believe there are things he is keeping quiet about."

"Everyone's entitled to his privacy."

"True, but when it starts to interfere with this lab and with one of my investigators, then that concerns me greatly." Caine reached across the table and grasped Lyra's hand. In all the years she'd worked for him, she could count on one hand the times he had touched her, offering her some sort of comfort or affection. "If you had information you knew would affect this case or about anyone working on this case, you would tell me, wouldn't you?"

"Of course," she said without hesitation, but her mind wandered to the warning Claire had given her.

He studied her for a long moment, then released his hold on her hand and sat back in his seat. "What do you think about Mistress Jannali? Do you think she's involved with this?"

Surprised at his question, Lyra frowned. Usually Caine didn't ask her for her opinion when it came to suspects and investigative paths to follow. He usually asked her about magic and spells, and areas he knew little about. Why was he asking her now?

"I don't know, but I do believe she's more than what we think she is."

"Why do you say that?"

"Because I think she can see the dead." Lyra rubbed her thumb over her amulet, finding comfort in the act. Nerves rang through her as she continued. "Gran put a protection spell over me when the mistress was here, and I think she heard Gran's voice and saw where her spirit was hovering over me."

"If that's true, what does that mean?"

"I can see Eleanore because she's tied to me spiritually, but no one else can see her, not unless the person has been between the world of the living and the world of the dead."

"What kind of creature can move between the two worlds?"

"Demons."

Both Lyra and Caine turned toward the door. Theron stood in the frame, looking tense and pensive.

"You think Ankara Jannali is a demon?" Caine asked, a look of incredulousness on his face.

Theron came fully into the room, but didn't take a

seat at the table. "I don't know. You asked what kind of creature can move between worlds, and I'm telling you that demons can."

"Do you care to elaborate on how you know that?"

"No, I do not."

Lyra stared at Theron. She knew how he knew about demons. It was so obvious but she didn't want to face it. Hadn't the psychic Claire warned her about it?

Theron practiced the dark arts. It had been staring her in the face the whole time—the book, his knowledge of demon summoning, his excess power and advance magic, and now his knowledge of demons. He practiced the very thing she abhorred. Why would Gran tell her to trust this man when he went against everything Lyra held dear in this world?

Caine glanced between Lyra and Theron, likely sensing the growing tension between them. "Remember to be at the mistress's home between nine and ten this evening."

"I'll be there," Lyra said.

"We'll be there together," Theron amended.

Caine nodded, then quickly left them alone.

Lyra stood, a hand on her hip and pointed at Theron. "You're a black practitioner."

"I was once, yes, but not anymore."

"You lied to me."

"No, actually I didn't. You never asked if I'd ever practiced the dark arts."

Anger and sorrow brought tears to her eyes. "An act of omission is just as bad as a lie." She wiped angrily at her tears, feeling foolish for believing in Theron. He wasn't the man she thought him to be, or wanted him to be.

"It was a long time ago, Lyra, and I learned from my mistakes."

"That doesn't make it okay."

"Maybe not, but I've paid the price for my misdeeds. And I won't be made to pay again."

The bitter, emotionless look he gave her made her take a few steps back. He didn't appear to be the same man she'd been kissing a mere twelve hours before. Gone was the devil-may-care glint in his eye and the confident yet alluring air that seemed to hover all around him. He had changed somehow, and Lyra wasn't sure when it had happened. Had she been blinded by her feelings for him?

"I can't believe you kept this from me, after everything we've been through."

"It should be obvious why I did."

"Well, it isn't. I guess I'm the dumb witch after all." Hurt beyond reason, she turned away from him, unable to keep looking at him without crying. She didn't want to give him her tears, too, after he had abused her trust.

"I knew you would react this way, Lyra. I knew you would look at me with disgust in your eyes. That's why I kept it from you, because I find it difficult to bear that one I care about would regard me in that way, as if I were unworthy."

Tears rolled down her cheeks. She didn't wipe them away. "If you truly cared about me, you would leave right now."

"I will leave, for now. But I'm not leaving Necropolis without dealing with this thing between us. We have something, Lyra, and I won't let you discard it because of my past."

She swung around to yell at him, to tell him there was nothing between them, nothing that could be resurrected after his admission, but he was already walking out the door.

Chapter 25

Theron waited at the doorway to the ballroom, scanning the crowd milling about in the foyer. Lady Ankara's centennial celebration was in full swing behind him, but he had no desire to partake in any festivities. Worry tightened his jaw as he waited for Lyra to appear.

He had called her house and her cell phone, but she hadn't answered either. He had arranged a car to take them to the party, but obviously she had no plans to arrive with him. She was angry at him, but he felt she was being foolish by operating on her own. No matter what she thought of him, she was still in danger. The woman was as stubborn as a mule.

Caine and Eve approached him, both dressed in their finery—Caine in a tux, Eve in an elegant black gown.

"I don't see Lyra. Is she with you?" Caine asked, craning his neck to look around the milling crowd.

"No. The witch is being obstinate."

"I told you not to leave her alone."

"I realize that, Caine, but the woman has a mind of her own."

The woman in question chose that very moment to arrive at the house. She pushed through the crowd to where they stood, and Theron lost all thought and reason.

She was a vision of magnificence in a flowing silk dress the color of newly budded leaves. Her hair was pinned up in a tousled auburn pile of loose curls. A few strands had already escaped to frame her pale oval face.

As Theron eyed her from head to toe, he realized that the dress she was wearing was the one from his dreams. Panic rushed through him and he wanted to wrap her safely in his arms and whisk her away from the party, from everything.

"You look lovely, Lyra." Eve took Lyra's hand and pulled her into a hug.

"Thank you," she said shyly, hardly sparing Theron a glance.

"We were worried about you," Caine said, his gaze flitting from Lyra to Theron.

She arched a brow, an exact duplicate of Caine's trademark look. "Were you?"

Theron cleared his throat, nerves clamping down on him. He kept his hands behind his back, so she couldn't see them shake. "Yes, I was supposed to escort you to the party and I've been unable to get hold of you. So, naturally, everyone was worried."

"Well, I'm fine."

"That's quite obvious." Theron rubbed at his chin. "You look spectacular, by the way."

The compliment threw her off, and she fidgeted at her

neckline, running her thumb over the talisman she always wore around her neck. She blushed. "Thank you." She gave him a once-over, then added, "So do you."

He bowed to her, and then offered her his arm. "Would you care to dance?"

She glanced at Caine and Eve, who shrugged, then back to Theron. "I don't dance."

"That dress was created for dancing. Please don't disappoint it."

Without a word, she took his arm and he drew her into the ballroom, through the crowd and onto the dance floor in the middle of the enormous, lavishly decorated room.

Keeping her hand, Theron set the other at her waist and twirled her around the floor to a traditional Viennese waltz. Although she claimed not to dance, she moved with grace, fluidly, like a meandering stream of fresh cool water.

Staring down at her as they moved around the room, he had to suppress the urge to kiss her, knowing she would taste like spring. Despite his hurt from her expected rejection, Theron still wanted her. He ached mind, body and soul for her. If only she could trust him for one more night. Maybe if he could sate his desire for her one time, he could move on and leave her to her anger. But he knew it wasn't possible. She'd never give him one night; he had hurt her too much, and he knew he couldn't leave after having her completely. He'd want more. Need more of the things she just wasn't willing to give him—not after betraying her trust.

"You dance beautifully," he commented, wanting to see her smile if only for a moment.

"I'm surprised I haven't stepped all over your feet."

"You have. I'm just wearing steel-toed shoes."

He was rewarded with a smile, and it lightened his heart to see it. He returned it and spun her around in a circle. Pulling her back in, the music slowed and he shifted his hand to her back and drew her close. He nuzzled his chin along the side of her head, reveling in the feel of her silky hair against his skin. She tensed under him, but he didn't pull away; he couldn't, not when he had her this close.

"I'm sorry for not telling you, Lyra," he murmured. "You never gave me a chance to apologize before, so I'm doing it now before you pull away from me again."

She flinched but didn't shrink from him. She shrugged. "I suppose I can understand why you didn't."

"Good."

"But it changes things between us."

"I know." He pressed his lips to the side of her head and drank in her scent, knowing this might be the last time he ever held Lyra close again.

"Can I cut in?"

Startled, Lyra pushed out of Theron's arms and swung around to gape at the icy beauty Nadja Devanshi as she stood off to the side eyeing them, a predatory gleam in her eyes.

Theron was about to protest when Lyra nodded. "Sure. I was hungry anyway." Without another word, she smiled then walked off the dance floor. Theron watched her leave, hoping she'd glance over her shoulder at him, but she didn't. She just disappeared into the streaming throng of partygoers.

Nadja settled herself into his arms, pressing her body close and cupping his neck. She was bold, the chanteuse. Theron had no misunderstanding of what she clearly wanted from him.

"I had hoped you would come to see me at the club," she said as she twirled a finger through his hair. "I thought it was clear I was available to you."

"It was clear, yes."

"We have much in common, you and I."

"Do we?"

She smiled and nuzzled her mouth against his neck. He could feel the brush of her fangs on his skin. He shivered, but not in pleasure. "You smell like power, Theron. We could do amazing things together."

"Like what?"

"Like change the world."

"I like the world just the way it is."

Nadja searched his face, then brushed her lips against his to whisper, "She's beneath you, the witch. You have better breeding than to soil yourself with her."

Theron stopped dancing and pushed Nadja away. Others on the dance floor stared at them. "I've only sullied myself by dancing with you."

Mouth gaping, Nadja glared at him. "How dare you speak to me like that? You forget your place, Theron LeNoir."

"I forget *nothing,* Nadja Devanshi. It's best *you* remember that."

Turning on his heel, Theron marched through the path the crowd opened for him to search for Lyra. He wiped at his mouth. The bitter taste of lavender remained on his lips. Had the vampiress poisoned him? Or used the same drug the mistress had used on him to induce strange visions? He couldn't be sure which.

It was now imperative for him to find Lyra and keep her safe. He had felt the malevolence radiating from Nadja, like a blast of cold, arctic wind. The woman had no heart—it had to have been frozen inside her rigid form. He'd met vampires like her before. Women who leeched onto men with power, their only purpose to literally suck them dry and use the power for their own nefarious purposes. His father, Lucien, had introduced him to people like that, when Theron had been practicing the dark magic. It was those people who sought to use the dark to gain whatever they could from it without a care about the consequences.

It was people like that whom he feared were now rallying in Necropolis around a dark practitioner to gain power. More power than even they knew existed, more than they could harness or control. Theron could sense a storm brewing. And at its center he feared only one woman stood to defy it—Lyra.

From across the room, Lyra had watched Theron dancing with the famous chanteuse. Jealousy stabbed her in the gut as they glided gracefully around the dance floor. Although she was angry at Theron and hurt that he had not told her about his dark past, she still couldn't help the treacherous pang in her heart. Her feelings for him hadn't changed. And that's what bothered her the most.

Not wanting to endure any more heartache, Lyra left the ballroom to do the job she had come to do.

Earlier, she had talked to Caine about their plan for the evening, and it was decided that Lyra's knowledge of an invisibility spell made her the best candidate to do the sneaking around.

Slipping into one of the many bathrooms in the house, Lyra locked the door, sat down on the lid of the toilet and concentrated. Closing her eyes, she murmured the words under her breath and clung on to the reserve of magical energy inside. Within moments, Lyra's skin began to tingle. Soon, a heated sensation surged over her body from the inside out. Another minute later, Lyra lifted her hands to her face and saw through them to the other side of the bathroom. The spell worked. She was invisible.

Carefully, she opened the door of the bathroom, hoping no one was standing there waiting. The area was clear and she stepped out into the hallway and made her way across the house to the room Theron said housed the mistress's collection. She didn't know if she'd find anything there, but it was a place to start. The mistress had shown Theron her things for a reason, or so everyone hoped.

Maybe they were just grasping at straws, anything to lead them to the killer. The team had been so thoroughly shut down at every corner they turned; maybe they were now seeing evidence and suspects in the shadows of those corners.

As she hustled down the hall, she peered into every room. The very last one contained Lady Ankara's collections and was the room she was looking for. Slipping inside, she partially shut the door and started to look around, searching for anything out of the ordinary.

She moved to the books in the corner first. Unassuming, three thick leather-backed texts sat on a shelf, a set of plain unadorned bookends keeping them pressed together. To a casual observer, the books would seem unimportant, especially compared to the items in the rest of the room, on display, spotlights pointing on them. The books had nothing to mark them as important, which was likely the idea.

She slid one volume out and right away noticed it

was the same book as Theron's. Setting that aside, she looked at the other two books. Both were old *grimoires,* spell books from an era Lyra couldn't decipher just from the text. The language used in some of the spells was old and unrecognizable. And she knew both Latin and some Aramaic.

After searching the books, Lyra moved around the room, along the back wall. In every display case she inspected, she saw nothing but the art inside. Finally, she came upon the statue Theron had said was over four thousand years old. She stared through the glass at the horned beast and wondered what it was about this piece that made the mistress show it to Theron.

Something glinted through the glass. Squinting, Lyra moved her head back and forth to see where it was coming from. It didn't seem to be glaring from the statue, but from beyond it. Stepping to the side, she looked around the display case and saw something metal flash on the floor along one wall.

Sidestepping the case, she hastily moved toward the wall and bumped a hip into another display case. This one didn't have any glass around it, and the vase sitting on top of the thin pillar started to wobble.

Lyra reached for the vase. Her fingertips brushed against it, but she failed to get a grip. As if in slow motion, the priceless porcelain vase fell to the ground. Cursing, she watched as it hit the floor.

It didn't break. But it did roll across the room hitting the back of the door and pushing it all the way shut. The noise of the lock engaging echoed in the room. There was no way the lycan standing guard down the hall hadn't heard it.

To make matters worse, Lyra raised her hands to her

face and realized the spell was starting to wear off. She could see the faint outline of her fingers.

Footsteps sounded down the hall. The guard was coming. She was going to get caught. She was going to lose her job—or worse.

In a panic, Lyra raced around the room looking for a place to hide. Scooping up the vase, she ran to the far side of the room, set the vase back onto its pillar and pressed into the shadows along the wall.

She sucked in a breath as the knob turned and the door opened. Her heart raced like wildfire and sweat soaked her back and chest. The lycan guard filled the doorway. His eyes glowed in the dark.

She was dead. He was going to see her.

"*Pardonez moi*, monsieur."

Lyra swore under her breath as she heard the French accent coming from the hallway. Theron. What was he doing?

The guard turned. "You're not allowed in this part of the house, sir."

"*Pardon. Pardon.* I seem to be a bit lost." His voice sounded slurred, his accent thick.

"You need to turn around and go back the way you came."

Through the open doorway, Lyra could see Theron slouching in front of the guard. Theron never slouched. She didn't think he even knew how to do that.

He put his arm around the guard. "I need to pee, *mon ami.*"

Theron was acting drunk. To her chagrin, it was the perfect distraction. She didn't want to be rescued. She hated that she needed him to get her out. Self-reliant for so long, she didn't want to need anything.

The guard tried to shrug Theron's arm off, but the dhampir was determined to keep it on. He succeeded in turning the lycan around so he was facing the hall and not the room. Unbelievably, Lyra saw the fingers on Theron's hand waving at her to make a move. To get out of the room.

Praying she was still see-through, Lyra quickly crossed the room and slipped out the door behind Theron and the guard.

"If you go back the way you came, sir, you'll find the bathroom."

"*Merci.* You are a good man." Theron's grin was lopsided. "You have many beautiful ladies here."

Lyra hugged the wall and quickly made her way past the distracted guard and down the hall. When she reached the corner, she broke into a run. She needed to get into a bathroom before the spell faded.

Finding the same bathroom she had changed in empty, she went in, shut the door and locked it. She ran water in the sink and splashed some on her face. She watched in the mirror as the enchantment faded and she became visible again.

Breathing another sigh of relief, she splashed more cold water on her cheeks then patted her face dry. She repinned her hair, smoothed down her dress, then opened the bathroom door to go back to the party and find Caine. Her mission had turned out to be a bust.

She'd failed. She'd never failed before. She'd always been good at what she set out to do. School, magic, crime-scene investigation. Now, she'd let the team down on something that should've been so simple to accomplish. And she hated that Theron had been there to see her fail, as well.

When she opened the door and walked out, she literally ran into Theron. He had been leaning against the door frame, waiting for her.

"Are you okay?" he asked.

She was relieved that she had escaped exposure, but she was angry that it had been Theron who had rescued her. She hated that he had known where she was and that she was in trouble.

It felt odd having someone, especially this man, know that much about her. He shouldn't know her so well. She hadn't given him permission to. This whole arrangement was unfamiliar and unnerving. And scary as hell.

"I'm fine." She brushed past him. "I didn't need your help."

He followed her behind. "That guard would've caught you if I hadn't come to the rescue."

"I didn't need rescuing. I'm not a damsel in distress, you know."

"Oh, you were in distress all right."

She whirled on him. "You've no right to save me, Theron. I didn't ask you to."

"No, you didn't, but I was there. You're just going to have to get used to that."

"What?"

"Me, being there for you. However much you dislike it, Lyra, I'm not leaving you alone. I told Caine I'd protect you, and I plan to."

She was so mad she could scream, but instead she bit down on her tongue and moved past him into the main ballroom.

He said nothing. He didn't need to. Lyra could see the lashes of pain she'd just inflicted on him all over his face. A knot twisted in her gut as he had stared at her, his jaw tight, his brow furrowed. Did he deserve her ire? Probably not, but at this point Lyra was beyond caring. She could feel her life spiraling out of control and she resented the fact that she wanted to reach out and hold on to Theron, knowing he possessed the power to stop her from spinning and keep her sane.

Chapter 26

Pained, Theron watched as Lyra marched through the crowded ballroom to the buffet table.

He knew that she had lashed out at him out of fear of almost being caught. And a recognition that she needed to be rescued. Lyra was a woman who prided everything on her independence, her strength and her ability to fend for herself. He just wished she knew he hadn't sought her out because he thought her weak or in need of his help. He had followed her, sensing her despite the invisibility spell, because of *his* desperate need to keep her safe. If anything happened to her, he would come undone. But the witch was way too stubborn to listen.

From a distance, he watched her pile decadent desserts onto a plate. Her lips were moving, but it appeared that she was speaking to the air because there was no one else near. He could just imagine the names she was calling him under her breath.

Despite her demand to leave her alone, he couldn't do it. Not with a clear conscience. He had vowed to keep her safe, and that was what he was going to do. Even if he had to protect her from herself.

Jace and Tala found Theron on the outskirts of the room, still watching as Lyra shoved chocolate pastries into her mouth.

"Where's Lyra?" Jace grunted.

Theron motioned toward the buffet. Scowling, Lyra was digging into what looked like chocolate mousse while she continued to speak into the air. "I believe she's angry with me."

Jace nodded as if that was the answer he was expecting. "Uh-huh. So, what did you do wrong?"

"I saved her from being caught while she was looking around a certain room."

Tala shook her head but said nothing.

"What did you do that for?"

Frowning, Theron looked at Jace. "Because I didn't want her to get caught."

"The girl's pretty resourceful. If she were in trouble she would've gotten out on her own."

"I thought she could use my help."

Jace slapped him on the back. "Well, you see, that's your number-one problem. Don't think."

"Yes, I'm starting to learn that." Theron straightened his shoulders and started to move in Lyra's direction. He was going to explain to her his intentions. He had to make her see that what he had done was for her own good.

But he didn't get very far before the lights in the ballroom dimmed and the crowd started to jostle and move back, pushing him with it.

Glancing around, he tried to see what was causing

the commotion. He knew there was to be entertainment, a floor show, but didn't think it would be so soon. Because of his height, Theron was still able to see the top of Lyra's head through the milling crowd. He focused on her, making sure he didn't lose sight of her.

The room went black as the eerie *thump thump thump* of a single drum reverberated off the walls. Heartbeats from the people surrounding him beat to the same rhythm in anticipation of what was to come.

Four colored spotlights flashed on, pointing in four different directions. One red light moved near Theron as the crowd parted to make way for a person walking on stilts. Covered by long, red, gauzy veils, the form headed to the center of the room, moving to the beat of the drums. For a moment, Theron watched the spectacle, just as mesmerized as everyone else by the visually stunning characters moving through the room, their stilts so tall it seemed as if they were walking on the air itself.

Theron had had the pleasure of seeing *Danse de la Lune* before when the acrobatic performing troupe had made an appearance in Nouveau-Monde. The show was spectacular, but his mind and gaze needed to be on Lyra. Shivers raced up and down his back. Something wasn't right. He could sense it all around him, despite the haunting music starting to play or the collective enthrallment of the swaying crowd.

Jostling for position, Theron craned his neck to peer over the heads of the crowd toward the buffet table. He couldn't see Lyra. Panic took hold of him. Heart racing, he pushed through the crowd, searching for her. Although the room was too dark and the crowd too big, he had to do something. He'd never forgive himself if something happened to her. He was supposed to be protecting her. Fine job so far, he thought, disgusted with himself.

Suddenly all the spotlights swiveled toward the center of the ballroom. Then the music changed. Instead of a rhythmic drumming, a haunting chorus of chanting voices reverberated through the room. The sound made the hair on the back of Theron's neck rise.

Next came a simple yet eerie tune played on a piano. And above it all came a single clear glass-breaking note sung in pure perfection. The sound put Theron's teeth on edge. He knew that voice. It could belong to only one person—Nadja Devanshi.

The moment she started to sing, he sensed something else at play. Power unlike anything he'd experienced before surged over the crowd like an electrical wave. It pushed and prodded at him, uncomfortably edging at his mind.

He had to get to Lyra now. There was something in the lyrics, a spell of some kind, and he was certain it was directed at his little witch.

As he moved past the guests, he noticed the looks of enthrallment on most faces. Some had tears streaking their cheeks. Whatever was in Nadja's song was affecting most of those in the room. Which, Theron figured, was the point.

Luckily, he'd learned to build up resistance to some of the more interesting vampiric traits. He had to, living with an overpowering, manipulative vampire with immense power. His father was a master of exploitation through whatever means he could use.

As Theron moved toward one of the exits, something made him stop. A cold breeze brushed over his skin and hair. The ends of his hair moved. He swiveled around to find the source of the breeze, but found nothing that could've made it.

Look and you will see.

The voice came from his left. He swiveled in that direction but found no one whispering in his ear.

Look! Turn around, Theron, and see.

Startled, Theron turned to his right, his gaze sweeping the open ballroom door, and his eye caught something of interest. A group of people were gathered in the hallway, all of their interest directed toward the floor. Then he caught sight of something that crushed the air from his lungs. A pair of green shoes and the silky green fabric of a dress.

Charging past the last of the crowd, he burst through the exit and rushed to the small murmuring group. He pushed past an elderly man to see Lyra lying unconscious on the floor, a woman on her knees patting Lyra's cheeks to try and rouse her.

Theron crouched next to her body and smoothed a hand over her forehead. "Lyra. Come, *ma chérie,* wake up."

She stirred under his touch. Eyelids fluttered open and he released the breath he had been holding when he saw recognition in her gaze.

"What happened?" she asked, her voice cracking.

Theron helped her sit and rubbed his hand up and down her back. "I'm not sure." He glanced around at the small crowd surrounding them.

The woman who had been kneeling next to Lyra spoke up. "I was coming from the washroom and found her lying on the floor."

"Was anyone around her?"

The woman shook her head.

As Theron helped Lyra to her feet, Caine and Eve came rushing out of the ballroom.

"Are you all right?" Caine asked, as he eyed her from head to toe.

Lyra nodded. "I'm fine. I have a headache is all."

"Do you know what happened?"

"I came out of the ballroom to get some air when the music started. That's the last thing I remember."

"Has she been spelled?" Caine asked Theron.

Theron looked Lyra over, placing his hand on her arm then moving it down to her hand. He shook his head. "I don't feel anything."

Lyra tried to shrug off his hand, but he held firm on to her. "I'm fine. Really. I just need to get out of here. Nadja's voice is making me sick."

"Were you able to find anything of use?" Caine asked.

Lyra shook her head, avoiding everyone's gaze. "No, I was interrupted before I could find anything. She does have the same book as Theron, though. The one with the symbols."

Caine nodded. "Okay, that might be enough to get a warrant."

"I'll take Lyra home. I have a car waiting at the door."

She glanced at him and must've seen the determination on his face because she didn't argue, but went along without comment.

Twenty minutes later, the car pulled up in front of Lyra's house. The driver got out and opened Lyra's door. She slid out without a word and walked, shoes hanging from a finger, up the walk and to the door. Theron followed her. He wasn't going to leave her alone, not now. Not with everything that had happened.

He needed to make sure she was safely tucked in bed before he'd let his guard down.

Without a backward glance, Lyra unlocked the door and walked in, leaving it open for Theron. Doing that brought down the magical wards surrounding her house, so he could enter without hindrance. He went in, locking it behind him. Dropping her shoes on the floor, she wandered across the living room and disappeared down the hall. He waited for her to come back out, but she didn't.

He waited five minutes before he moved down the hallway. He passed the bathroom. The door was open but Lyra wasn't inside. He continued to another open doorway—her bedroom.

Stopping at the threshold, he peered into the room. Lamplight revealed Lyra sitting on her bed, staring at her feet. She didn't look up when he moved farther into the room.

"Are you okay?"

She nodded.

He sat on the edge of the bed, next to her. "Is there anything I can get you?"

She glanced at him and frowned. "I'm sorry for the way I acted earlier."

"It's okay."

"It's your fault anyway." She ran her foot over the carpet, making a design in the fibers.

"Is it now?"

"Yes. I feel so out of control when I'm near you." She sighed. "No one's made me feel that way before. I don't like it."

"Well, if it's any consolation, you drive me insane, too."

Her lips lifted into a smile and she nudged him with her elbow. "Great, so we both drive each other nuts. So what are we going to do about it?"

"Give in."

Cupping her around the neck, Theron leaned in and touched his lips to hers. It was gentle, hesitant at first. But when she moaned, he deepened it, sweeping his tongue into her mouth.

Lifting her hands, she buried them in his hair and held on as he took her mouth. Teeth, tongue, lips. He couldn't get enough of her. She tasted like the champagne she had sipped and a fresh cool breeze. Refreshing, invigorating. She made his heart race and his stomach flip over. No other woman had been able to elicit such sensations from him before.

Nibbling on her bottom lip, he then pressed kisses to her chin, over her neck to her ear, where he knew she liked to be caressed. With his tongue, he made little circles just under her earlobe. He was rewarded with her quick gasps of pleasure.

"Theron," she panted.

Lifting his head, he cupped her cheeks and stared into her eyes. "Please don't ask me to stop. I won't be able to bear it."

"Then don't." She nipped at his lips. "I'm yours."

Covering her mouth with his, he ran his hands over her back. He needed to touch her skin now. To feel the silkiness of her flesh beneath his palms.

His fingers found the zipper at the back of her dress and although impatient to feel her, he slowly pulled it down, torturing himself. Once open, he gripped the two edges and slid them down, off her shoulders and down her arms. Her breath caught in her throat as she pulled her arms out of the dress. A thin, silky camisole, the color of emeralds, covered her breasts.

Theron leaned down and pressed his lips to her shoulder, trailing his tongue along her collarbone to her other shoulder. Lyra let her head fall back as he nibbled and tasted the hollow of her throat and worked his way down.

The lace of the camisole flirted at the swell of her breasts. Pushing it away with his tongue, Theron edged down lower still. He could feel her heart race under the press of his mouth.

Hooking his fingers around the straps of her camisole, he pulled them down. Achingly slow, he revealed more of her flesh. Inch by inch, he moved the fabric down to finally reveal her perfect pale breasts.

"Magnifique." Blushing, she raised her arms to cover herself. Theron set his hands on top of hers. "You are too beautiful to hide, *ma petite sorcière.*"

Holding her hands, he brought them down to her sides, then kissed her, slowly taking her down to the mattress. Shuffling her in toward the middle of the bed, he settled in beside her, kissing and nibbling on her delicious mouth.

Sitting up, he gripped the edges of her dress and slid it the rest of the way off. Underneath, she wore only a matching pair of green cotton panties. He drank her in, memorizing every detail of her stunning body—every curve and slope. He wanted to press his mouth to every part of her, to taste her creamy skin on his tongue.

She reached for him, and he linked his hands with hers. "I want to see you, Theron. Every part of you."

Chapter 27

Smiling, he released her hands and unbuttoned his shirt. Shrugging out of it, he tossed it theatrically on the floor. She smiled, loving how he made her feel so at ease with his playfulness. It also helped that she was still feeling the effects of the alcohol she had consumed. It lowered her defenses, lessened her inhibitions. She gloried in the feeling of being able to free herself to Theron.

The light from her bedside lamp played over the rippling muscles of his chest. From the way he carried himself and the lithe way he moved, Lyra knew he'd be lean and powerful, but she had no real idea until now.

His chest was muscular, defined, with hard, washboard abs. She wanted to trace her finger over every ridge and dip. A light sprinkling of dark hair lined his sternum leading down to the waistband of his trousers.

Hesitant, yet feeling bold, Lyra lifted her hand and

feathered a finger down the path. The skin covering his steel-like muscles was smooth but the hair under the pad of her finger was prickly. Theron shuddered under her touch and she smiled, feeling the power of her stroke. She wondered what other sensations she could pull from him using only her fingers.

Sitting up, and keeping her gaze on his, she unbuttoned his pants and lowered the zipper. Her hands shook as she tugged at the fabric, freeing his erection. Taking in a deep breath, she glanced down at him and sighed.

Not knowing what to expect, she found him more beautiful than she thought he'd be. She'd seen men before in magazines but never experienced the same thrill she was feeling now. Maybe it was because it was Theron. He made all the difference in the world.

"Touch it, Lyra." His voice was low and thick with desire.

She did as he asked and wrapped her hand around his shaft. He groaned harshly the second she made contact. Lyra reveled in her power to elicit such a response, from a simple touch of her hand on his cock. He was like velvet steel, hard and soft at the same time. Curious, she explored the rest of his rigid length. She touched, caressed and massaged every inch of him until he grabbed her hand, stilling her movements.

"Enough," he growled.

Keeping her hand in his, he pressed her back onto the bed, taking her mouth once again. When he swept his tongue over hers, tasting, teasing with every stroke, it was her turn to groan. She could kiss him for hours.

After one more thorough caress of her lips, Theron sat back and tore his pants the rest of the way off. Kneeling beside her hip, he ran his hands over her breasts, flicking her nipples with his thumbs. Jolts of electric heat surged over her as he rubbed her taut peaks, pulling and pinching.

Leaning down, he swirled his tongue over one nipple then the other. He did it over and over, alternating between the two, giving each one equal heated attention, until she was mewling in rapture. Finally, he wrapped his lips around one of her breasts and suckled on her. With every pull on his mouth, she felt an answering tug between her thighs. She was like a ticking time bomb, ready to explode.

Relinquishing his hold on her nipple, Theron sat up and ran his hands over her stomach and down her thighs. With each stroke, she lifted her hips, arching into his touch. She was on fire. Liquid heat swirled at her center. She was going to burn from the inside out if he didn't hurry and quench her smoldering desire.

Keeping his eyes on her face, he hooked his fingers into the band of her panties. Breath catching, she gasped as he slowly eased them over her hips and down her legs. When they were completely off, Theron caressed her with his eyes and his hands. He went on a slow ascent of her legs, from her ankles to her thighs. When his thumbs brushed the sensitive inner skin between her legs, she jolted off the bed.

"I'm burning. Oh Goddess, I can't handle it." Aching, she wrapped her hands around his arms, unsure what she wanted him to do. Fast, slow, she couldn't decide. The hot sensations he created in her body left her spinning, whirling out of control.

"Hold on, *bien-aimée*. I won't hurt you."

Nodding, she dug her fingers into his arms. She trusted him with her body, and with her heart. She knew he'd never intentionally hurt her. Not now, not ever.

Knocking her legs apart with his knee, he knelt between them, keeping his hands on her hips, rubbing his thumbs in circles over her skin.

"Bend your knees for me, Lyra. I want to see all of you."

His words inflamed her even more. She didn't think it was possible to feel so wanton, so lustful, from a few kisses and soft caresses. But it was the craving she saw in Theron's eyes that completely took her under desire's spell. He wanted her so badly—that made her feel even more desirable.

Hesitantly, she brought her knees up, feeling open and vulnerable. But at the same time, it revved her up, made her sex ache with need that much more.

Sitting back, Theron's gaze traveled over her. Down her torso over her hips, to the center of her need. Biting her lip, she watched as his eyes drank her in. The color of his eyes darkened, and the look on his face was one of longing and hunger.

"Ma petite *sorcière,* so beautiful."

He trailed his fingers from her knee down her thigh, feathering light caresses to her skin. Her flesh vibrated as he neared her sex. She sucked in a breath as he slid a finger over her mound and slipped inside her soft folds.

Jolts of pleasure surged over her. She'd never felt anything so sensory before, so intense. She arched her back as he stroked her. Battering at her senses, more fervent delight jolted her system. She rode the wave while Theron caressed her more, and then boldly glided a finger into her heat.

She cried out, tangling her hands into the sheets on the bed. More pleasure washed over her as he stroked and manipulated her, adding another finger, alternating between fast and slow. She was dizzy by the time she realized he had removed his fingers and was nuzzled against her opening.

With one hand he pushed her leg back, spreading her wide. The other hand slowly worked the round knob of his erection back and forth along her slick folds. Biting her lip, she arched her back urging him further. However much she knew it would hurt, she wanted him inside.

"Relax, darling. I'll go slow." He spoke through gritted teeth.

She could tell he was struggling with restraint. His arms shook and sweat rolled down his face to drip onto her belly. It was an obvious effort for him to not ram into her body, yet he took care to go slow. Could she push him far enough that he would lose control? Did she possess the power to drive him mad? The tantalizing thought filtered through her mind. She hoped to find out.

With a slow, practiced stroke, he inched into her then stopped. She released her breath, allowing her body to adjust to him. She wondered when she would feel the pain. All she felt was glorious pleasure surging through her with each careful press of his shaft inside her body.

Leaning forward, he pushed a little more of himself into her. She gripped his shoulders, digging her fingers in. "I won't break, Theron. I promise."

Clamping his eyes shut, he fell forward and drove the rest of the way into her. Something inside her ripped and she felt a stab of pain flare through her thighs and over her belly.

Reaching between them, Theron slid his fingers over her, caressing her gently, easing her pain. His thumb found the sensitive bundle of nerves and rubbed her there. The pain receded and only pleasure washed through her.

She wrapped her arms around him as he started to move inside her. Slow at first, then harder, faster, until he rode her hard. Moving his head, he found her mouth and kissed her hard. For every stroke of his tongue he matched it with each thrust inside her core. Hooking her legs over his hips, she arched up to meet him.

He buried his hands in her hair as he drove into her, taking her to the edge. Nibbling along her jaw, she could feel the scrape of his fangs on her skin. It made her shiver with a different type of pleasure. To know he could use them on her, to sink them into her and taste her blood. It was decadent and dangerous. That she could feel that with a man, *this* man, and still feel safe, was an exhilarating sensation.

"Ma sorcière," he panted into her ear. "Mine." Then buried himself deep, to her womb.

Crying out, she raked her nails over his back. A different type of heat radiated over her, from her, from him. It was similar to what she sensed when they had mingled their magic together to make a spell. Energy surged through her, over her and onto him. Back and forth the force went, around and over every part of their bodies, covering them both in a heated layer of power.

Writhing underneath Theron's powerful form, Lyra sensed she was near the verge. She could hardly breathe, she could hardly think. She could only feel. Every nerve ending in her body fired, every cell seemed to explode, every muscle clenched, ready to tumble over the edge into oblivious rapture.

With every drag and pull, each thrust, she drew closer and closer, until finally everything around her exploded into a blinding white ball of light. Squeezing her eyes shut, Lyra screamed as she came in an eruption of sensory overload.

"Oh, Theron. Oh Goddess, yes!" she cried as she squeezed her legs around him, milking him, trying desperately to hang on as her orgasm took her under in a wave of heat and pleasure.

Gripping her tight around the shoulders, Theron pumped once then twice, then slammed into her, burying his face into her neck, and came. She felt every powerful surge, as he emptied himself inside her.

She didn't know how long it was before she could think, let alone move. Breathing hard, she ran a hand over Theron's back, enjoying the feel of his sweaty skin. He groaned, then lifted himself off her to roll onto his back. His arm was over his face and he groaned again.

"Are we alive?" he asked, his breath fanning her neck, coming out in harsh gasps.

With her breath mimicking his, she whispered, "I don't know. Maybe."

Removing his arm, Theron glanced at her and smiled. He tugged on her, drawing her close into the crook of his arm. Once there, he stroked her arm with his fingers, then found her mouth with his. He kissed her so thoroughly it made her toes curl all over again.

She raised her hand to play with the hair on his chest. It felt leaden and she giggled at the tingles in her muscles. "Are you supposed to feel like Jell-O afterwards?"

Theron kissed the tip of her nose. "Only if you do it right."

Yawning, Lyra snuggled in closer. It felt right being here with Theron. As if she fit perfectly alongside him, filling in a missing piece. She couldn't believe that she fought it for so long, when the easiest thing to do was to give in to the magic they made together.

She yawned again. "I'm sorry for yelling at you."

"It's okay. I probably deserved it."

"But you didn't. I'm just so…so used to doing things for myself, being on my own. I didn't know what to do with your concern for me. It scared me."

He squeezed her shoulder and kissed her nose again. "I know. It scares me, too."

She ran her hand over his chest, loving the way his muscles bunched and flexed under her touch. She could spend the rest of her life right here, in the crook of Theron's arm, feeling safe and secure…and loved.

"We can make it work, right? There's something powerful between us, isn't there?"

He lifted her chin with a finger and nodded. "Yes. I'm not going anywhere, Lyra. I'm right here for as long as you want me to be."

"Promise?"

"Yes."

He pressed his lips to her temple and murmured against her skin, "I want to explain everything to you, so there's nothing keeping us apart."

She looked him in the eye, knowing he referred to his dark past. She smiled, letting him know she was ready to hear it.

With fingers trailing up and down her arm, for both their comfort, he told her everything he'd been keeping inside.

"I started playing around with spells strictly to test my growing skills. I came into my magic late and didn't have anyone to guide me. Lucien didn't allow me much contact with my mother."

Lyra could feel him tense as he spoke. She stroked a hand over his chest to soothe him.

"It's not an excuse for my behavior but a reason why I was drawn to the power of the dark magic. My father has always been an overriding influence in my life. Pushing me, goading me into being more than everyone else. Power was one thing he respected. And I suppose, like all young sons, I desperately wanted his respect."

"You were raised as a vampire. It's understandable," Lyra added, hoping to ease his pain even just a little.

"I started with small spells, simple incantations that allowed me to acquire the things I desired, in business and with women. After a time, I had a small following who were seduced by my increasing power." His eyes glossed over as he spoke the next words. "Jenna was so innocent, so trusting and so in love with me she'd do anything I asked of her. I was an ignorant fool to agree. Drunk on power, I had no clue that we were invoking the darkest of spells, that there would be a price to pay. I could feel the heat of the magic inside me. It was so seductive that I wanted to share it with her. But she wasn't near ready for it—she was too inexperienced. When I forced it from my body into hers, I had no idea what it would do." He raised his hand to his face and stared at it. "Her hands burned up so quick, like kindling in a fire. There was nothing I could do to stop it. I can still hear her screams in my dreams."

Tears streaked down his cheeks. Lyra reached up and wiped them away with the tips of her fingers. He met her gaze and she could see the torment in his eyes. He suffered every day for his past mistakes.

"What happened to her?"

He dropped his hand to his side. "She lives in Vienna. She married the doctor who worked on her hands. They have two beautiful children." His lips lifted into a sad smile. "She's a painter now. Her hands have been reconstructed. She'd actually quite good. I have a couple of her pieces in my home."

"It sounds like she's forgiven you."

"She has."

"Then you need to forgive yourself, Theron." Reaching for him, she kissed him. She could sense the relief in him as she feasted on his lips. She felt it, too.

Closing her eyes, she felt tears brimming in the corners. She wanted to smack herself for wasting so much time hating Theron when in fact she had been in love with him from the very start. His dark past no longer disturbed her, because she knew now how much of a different man he had become. He wasn't perfect— that was for sure. He had his flaws, certainly—but underneath it all, she knew him to be a moral and compassionate man. Someone she could love for a lifetime.

Playing with the hair at his navel, she said sleepily, "It's my birthday tomorrow."

He pressed his lips to hers and murmured, "Happy birthday, *ma petite sorcière.*"

She smiled against his lips. He kissed her again until, yawning again, she cuddled against his chest and fell asleep.

Again Theron was on the dark city street, hunkering down in the shadows waiting for Lyra to walk into the yellow glow of lamplight.

An icy breeze blew up where he waited, swirling trash and debris around his head. He had to lift a hand to shield his eyes from the flying dirt. That hadn't happened before.

There was something inherently different about this dream. Before he couldn't feel his surroundings. He didn't feel the bite of the cold night air or the unyielding hardness of the cement beneath his feet.

This time he experienced everything as if it were truly reality and not a dream.

But he was still asleep, wasn't he? Curled next to Lyra after making love?

He waited a little longer before he realized she wasn't coming. Something had happened.

As he moved out of his hiding spot, he spied another form walking down the middle of the street. It wasn't Lyra, but another woman—an older woman with the same auburn hair and striking chestnut eyes.

"Theron LeNoir," she called. "I have a message for you."

He stepped into the road and walked toward her. The moment she noticed him, she smiled and raised her hand to him.

"Who are you?" he demanded, suddenly afraid, but not of the woman.

"Search your soul and you will know who I am."

He didn't have to think long. He knew who the woman was; he could see Lyra in her eyes. "Eleanore."

She nodded. "I have an urgent message for you."

Theron's whole body quaked in fear. Something dark was happening. He could feel it rushing through his veins like poison.

"Together you can make it right. Together you are strong. Together your magic can go from dark to light, make things right from wrong."

He shook his head. "I don't understand."

"You will when the time is right. Now, wake up,

Theron." Her gaze bore into him. Violent shivers rushed over him again, but he tried to shrug them off.

"Wake up! *She's been taken!*"

Chapter 28

Jolting from sleep, Theron blinked back the light streaming in through the window he faced. He put a hand to his chest where his heart hammered. The dream had been so real. Eleanore's voice still rang in his ears.

Feeling groggy and fogged over from sleep, he turned to look for Lyra, feeling the need to hold her close. He flipped over but found the spot where she had lain empty.

He sat up and scanned the room. His head spun. Had he been drugged? "Lyra?"

No answer.

Heart racing, he yanked back the bedcovers and jumped out of the bed, rushing into the adjourning bathroom. Maybe she was showering. The stall was empty, and no residual water dripped from the tap.

Panic gripped him tight, making it difficult to

breathe. He rushed down the hall, peering into the other bathroom and found it empty, too. He continued to the living room and kitchen. Again, no Lyra.

The room was spinning. Grabbing the phone, he sat on the sofa and dialed her cell phone number. It rang. He could hear the shrill cry coming from her purse, which was sitting on the kitchen counter where she had set it the night before. Disconnecting, he dialed the lab.

Caine answered on the third ring. "Valorian."

"Have you seen Lyra?" he asked, trying to keep the panic from his voice.

But the vampire must've heard it regardless. "What's happened?"

"Lyra's gone." He paused, unsure of how to say what was in his mind. "I think they've taken her."

"Where are you?"

"At Lyra's."

"Stay there. We're coming. Don't touch anything else. Her house is a crime scene now."

After setting the phone down, Theron didn't know what to do. Caine had told him to stay put and not do anything, but how could he when the woman he loved had been kidnapped?

He loved Lyra. The realization didn't hit him over the head like a sledgehammer. He had known it for some time; he just hadn't had the guts to admit it to himself, or to her.

Now he might never get the chance.

After glancing at the clock in the kitchen, Theron saw it was late afternoon. He didn't think they would perform the ceremony until full dark, midnight most likely, to obtain the best conduit to the dark side of magic. So the team had a little over seven hours to find her. He hoped it would be enough.

After slipping on his pants, Theron paced the living room, trying to figure out how someone could've gotten past Lyra's wards and taken her without waking him. It had to have been a spell of some kind.

Realization slammed him in the gut. The lavender. Nadja's kiss. The spell had been on her lips and she had transferred it to him when she had kissed him. Instinctively, he had licked his lips afterward, hadn't he? Taking the spell into his mouth.

It was so much like Lady Ankara's hallucinatory spell. But this one obviously had tagged him, allowing the follower to find him and enter Lyra's house without worrying about the wards. And it had successfully knocked him out so Lyra could be taken without waking him. A dark spell for certain.

A knock came at the door. Theron opened it, ushering in Caine and the rest of the team. They had made it in less than twenty minutes.

Setting down his kit, Caine had already snapped on latex gloves. He scanned the living room. Without looking at Theron, he asked, "Where was she when she was taken?"

"In bed."

Caine looked at him then. "Where were you?"

Theron arched a brow, not wanting to get into it with the vampire. He was supposed to be a great investigator; he could figure it out on his own.

Eve stepped in between them. "Enough of the macho crap." She had an ink blotter in her hand. "I'll need to take your prints, Theron, so we can distinguish them from the kidnappers'."

Nodding, he let her do her job. When she finished, he wandered into the bedroom where the others were taking pictures, dusting for prints and collecting fibers. There was nothing he could help with. He felt useless, impotent even.

Jace glanced at him when he stepped into the room, a look of hostility planted on the lycan's face. He knew the look, the one that told him point blank that Jace thought it was his fault Lyra had been taken. He swallowed it without protest. Because the lycan was right.

It *was* his fault.

"Tell me what happened last night," Caine said from his position by the window. He'd just finished dusting for prints on the glass and ledge. He then added, "Only the relevant stuff, please. I don't need to know the rest."

"I believe Nadja Devanshi spelled me, enabling her, or whoever invoked the spell, to break Lyra's wards and take her from her bed while I was put under."

"How do you know?"

"The lavender. I tasted it on my lips after she kissed me. It veils the tartness of other potions, the kind that could've done what I just described."

"Nadja had an alibi for Lori James's murder. She was at the club. She's not the one murdering people."

"Or she's not acting alone," Theron offered.

"The mistress?" Caine asked.

Theron nodded. "The lavender tea I had at her home also masked a potion I drank. One she used to try and blackmail me about certain events in my past."

"What kind of events?" Jace asked.

"The kind that makes me very familiar with the spells put on me and with the ceremony that is sure to happen at midnight, if we don't hurry and find Lyra."

"Black magic," Caine said.

"Yes."

Everyone was staring at him now. He was certain every one of them wanted to hurt him in some way, for losing one of the team, losing someone so important to them. Little did they know that Lyra was now the most essential person in his life, as well. By the looks in their eyes, he didn't think they'd listen or care.

"Why Lyra?" Caine asked.

"Because Lyra is the final piece in this puzzle. She's the sacrificial virgin they need to complete the ceremony and open the portal to hell. Literally." He sighed. "But they will discover that Lyra is not a virgin any longer and I'm not sure how they will react."

"Why tonight?"

"Because it's her birthday."

Caine closed his eyes and swore. Eve grabbed his hand and squeezed it. "How long have you known this?" he bit out through a clenched jaw.

Theron met his gaze, owning up to his mistake, his omission that might cause the woman he loved to die. "For a couple of days now. That's why I volunteered to be her bodyguard. I knew they would eventually come after her. I wanted to keep her safe."

"Fine job you did there, asshole," Jace growled, as he got to his feet from his crouch near the bed. Clenching his hands, he started toward Theron, murder flashing in his eyes. "I'm going to rip you apart for this."

Caine grabbed the lycan by the arm. "Jace. Stop. That won't help, however much it might feel good to do."

"May I suggest you keep your anger under control until after we find Lyra?" Theron said. "Then you may *try* and rip me apart if you like."

"Oh, I like," Jace grunted.

Caine glanced at his watch. "Okay, we're on a time clock, people. Let's get all the evidence we have back to the lab to process. Lyra's counting on us to do our jobs right."

"Do we really have time to process evidence, Caine? I think it's obvious who has Lyra," Theron said, anxiety racing through him. He hated standing here doing nothing, when he knew exactly where they were keeping Lyra.

"If the mistress is behind this, we need all the evidence we can get to convict her. Politics won't be on our side in this one."

"Does it really matter at this point?" Theron asked. "A conviction? Do you really think you're going to get one even if you have the evidence? This city is run by Ankara and vampires like her. I'll bet half of them are even a part of this." He ran a hand over his face, exasperation making his hands shake. "It's a quest for power, Caine, by those with power."

Caine stared at Theron. He knew Theron was right. Being a vampire himself, he knew exactly what went on behind the scenes. He had to know that no matter what they found to convict the mistress of a crime, she wouldn't be going to jail or in front of a jury. The law wasn't going to work for them this time.

Mahina marched into the bedroom. "I found a witness who saw a black sedan parked on the street around three a.m."

"Did they happen to get a license plate?" Caine asked, his voice tinged with the hope everyone else was certainly feeling.

The lycan police captain grinned. "Oh yeah, they did.

I got it, and already ran it. Guess who it belongs to?" She paused, glancing at her notebook. "Jerome Spindler, Lady Ankara Jannali's assistant and jack-of-all-trades, including kidnapper."

After Mahina's announcement, Caine glanced at everyone, meeting each of their gazes. Theron could see the cold fury on the vampire's face. It reflected his own.

"If we do this and we're wrong, it could mean our jobs." He put his arm around his wife. "I need to know if everyone is okay with that. If you're not, you can stay out of it. No one will think any less of you."

"I'm in," Eve said without hesitation. Theron wasn't surprised. He had heard about her kidnapping after the first set of murders.

"We're in." Tala grabbed Jace's hand and squeezed. Jace nodded.

Mahina tucked her notebook into her inner jacket pocket. "You don't even have to ask, Valorian."

Caine's gaze settled on Theron. He could feel the vampire trying to read him. Theron relaxed and let him in. He had nothing to hide anymore.

"Do you love her?"

"Yes."

"Are you willing to do whatever it takes to get her back?"

"Yes."

Caine nodded, satisfied. "Okay. We need a game plan." He rubbed a hand over his chin. "It's too bad the baron is such a coward. His consent actually might help in this situation."

A second later, Laal walked into the bedroom. "I came as fast as I could." He patted at his hair, which was in disarray and not slicked back as usual. "I have a

message from Rick. He says the DNA belongs to Ankara Jannali. That was what Gwen found out."

Caine smiled.

"Is there anything else I can do?" Laal asked.

"Do you know any judges who aren't members of the
club?"

The baron nodded. "Judge Mica Smith. She's a lycan
and surly as hell, but fair."

"Good. Call her. We're going to need all the help
we can get."

Chapter 29

When Lyra woke, her body was shaking so violently she couldn't keep her teeth from chattering. Blinking back tears, she opened her eyes to darkness and cold. She definitely was not tucked in her bed in the crook of Theron's arm.

Feeling around with her hand, she realized that she was on her side on a cement floor. There was nothing near her that she could discern. No bed, no chair, nothing to identify where she might be.

Rolling onto her back, she knew with certainty that she'd been kidnapped. They had finally gotten to her. But how? Theron had been with her. Images of their lovemaking flashed through her mind.

Her hands went to her body. Relief surged over her when she realized that she was clothed and not naked as she'd been when she went to sleep. Thankfully, whoever had kidnapped her had had the decency to dress her in what felt like a robe.

How had they gotten through her wards? And why didn't Theron wake up? Maybe they had subdued him first, but then she would've felt it, wouldn't she? Unless they had inside help to break her magic.

She squeezed her eyes shut against the alarming thought that Theron had something to do with this. That he hadn't given up his dark ways and had been working on her, gaining her trust, the whole time.

She shook her head as tears rolled down her cheeks to drip on the floor beneath her. No. She wouldn't believe it. Theron loved her. She would've sensed his betrayal. Her gran would never have told her to trust him if that had been the case. She would've known the truth about him.

The last thing she needed to do was to confuse her mind with conspiracy theories and useless thoughts about what could have been. She needed her wits about her if she was going to get out of here alive.

"Gran?" Her voice echoed back to her.

There was no response.

Lyra put her hands out, feeling for her grandmother's essence. Her skin was left cold.

"Gran? This is no time to give me the silent treatment." The desperation in her voice bounced back to her from the emptiness of the room. It sounded hollow.

Pushing to a sitting position, Lyra forced her eyes to adjust to the darkness. After blinking several times, outlines of the walls appeared. She was definitely in a large room without any furnishings. Nothing seemed to be on the walls, either. Squinting harder, she could make out the outline of a rectangular fixture along one wall. Unsure of what was above her, she crawled toward it.

As she neared it, she could distinguish more shape and a possible color. It was a large, whitish, box-type unit. She pressed her hand to it. The outside was plastic-coated and cold. Standing, she ran her hands over it and found something that felt like a handle on top. She pulled with all her strength. The lid gave way. An icy puff of air rushed over her. Heart racing, she lowered her hand and touched ice.

She dropped the lid. It slammed shut with a rever-berating snap. It was a freezer. A large one. The one she suspected Theron had seen in his vision, the one that had held Lori James's body.

Cowering along the floor again, Lyra couldn't stop her hands and body from quivering. Fear tightened its grip on her. She could barely breathe from the pressure on her chest. She had to get out of here.

Swiveling to scrutinize the room, she could make out the outline of a door. It was about six feet to her left. She crawled to where she thought it was located. The closer she got, the more she could see the definitive shape of the door and the handle to open it. She put her hand out and touched it when she neared.

It burned like fire. She snatched her hand back and blew on the seared flesh of her fingertips. There was magic on the door—a powerful ward to prevent her from opening it. She should've suspected as much.

The wards also likely prevented her from contacting her gran. For the first time in her life, she was truly and utterly alone.

Scooting away from the door, Lyra leaned against the adjacent wall to think. Thankfully, she hadn't been drugged, as Eve had been when she was taken. She was surprised about that. It was for a reason, though—that much she knew for certain. Maybe they needed her awake and aware for whatever they had planned for her.

Fear strangled her as she considered what was going to happen. She now knew the last part of the symbols and text in the book, the final ceremony. She mentally slapped herself for not figuring it out sooner.

She was to be the final sacrifice, the Virgin Mary for their hellish birth.

Oh, they were going to be so mad when they found out that she wasn't a virgin anymore. Somehow, she didn't think it would stop them from killing her, though. Her execution had been scheduled, she had no doubt.

Midnight most likely. The last hour of her birthday. She hoped it would be enough time for Theron and the others to find her.

Happy birthday to me. Fighting tears, she rubbed her hands over her face. How long did she have? She had no idea what time it was, or if it was day or night. She could be a few minutes away from her death sentence and not know it.

Images of Theron flashed through her mind. Their night together had been amazing. She'd never experienced such raw emotions and sensations before. It was as if he had ripped her open and melded with her both physically and spiritually. Even now, she could feel his magic on her skin and deep inside her soul.

Pulling on that energy, Lyra wrapped it around her body and fed from its warmth. Theron's scent wafted to her nose. She clamped her eyes down on more tears as she inhaled his essence. If she concentrated, she could actually feel his arms around her, embracing her tightly.

What she wouldn't give to be there now, in her bed, in his arms, listening to his rhythmic breathing and the steady beat of his heart. His good heart. She wished she'd taken the chance to tell him, that she hadn't been such a coward to open herself up. Now, she might never get the opportunity to tell him she loved him.

The door creaked open. Scuttling back, Lyra watched in horror as a cloaked form filled the doorway.

"Hello, witch. It's time we formally meet." It was a woman's voice coming from the black shroud.

Gathering all her energy, Lyra formed a binding spell between her hands and tossed it. It fizzled within a foot from where she crouched on the floor.

The dark figure laughed. "Your magic is useless here. I've had this whole room warded."

"What do you want?"

"What do you think I want, you silly girl?" She stepped farther into the room. "I want you to die."

The figure pounced on Lyra so quickly, she didn't have time to scream.

Chapter 30

Two hours later and armed with a search warrant, Theron and the members of the OCU were knocking on Mistress Jannali's front door. It hadn't taken much convincing for Judge Smith to grant the warrant. She seriously hated the mistress anyway. At the same time, Monty and his people were executing another warrant at Nadja Devanshi's home. Hopefully, someone would find Lyra alive.

A uniformed servant opened the door. "Yes?"

Mahina held the warrant to the elderly man's face. "We have a warrant to search the premises."

He took it with shaking hands and licked his lips nervously, then glanced at the seven faces staring in at him.

"Is the mistress home?" Caine asked.

The servant shook his head.

"Could you please step out of the house, sir?" Mahina held the door open for him to step out.

Once he came out, the lot of them went in, gathering as a group in the main foyer. Theron's nerves were on fire. He couldn't stand still. He started down the hallway, but Caine grabbed his arm, stopping him from going any farther.

"Trust me, Theron. I know how you're feeling right now, but we need to be smart and search thoroughly."

Theron nodded, but shrugged off Caine's hand. He was too wired to have anyone touching him. The only person whose skin he wanted to feel was Lyra's.

"This place is huge, so we'll need to split up," Caine suggested. "Jace and Tala, you two take the west wing. Mahina and Laal, you take the upstairs. Theron, you're with me and Eve. We'll search this wing."

Faces grim, everyone nodded.

"Turn your radios on. I don't have to tell any of you how urgent this is. If you find anything, and I mean anything, call it in. Lyra's counting on us."

Mahina and Laal took the stairs quickly, and were at the top before the rest of them could get moving.

Jace walked to Theron, his jaw tight and his eyes guarded. He offered Theron his hand. Surprised, Theron took it. "We'll find her."

Theron nodded, too overcome with emotion to speak.

After one final shake of his hand, Jace let go and went back to where Tala was waiting for him. Grasping hands, they made their way down another hallway toward the west wing.

Caine glanced at Theron. "Let's go."

Without waiting for Caine or Eve, Theron ran down

the side hall to the collection room. He flicked on the lights, searching the room for any indication of Lyra's presence. He rushed to the Egyptian statue the mistress had shown him, peering into the glass case. The answer had to be here somewhere.

Something flashed at him through the glass. Side-stepping the display case, Theron charged toward the wall. He crouched down and touched something metal. It looked like a locking mechanism.

"I found something," he shouted.

Caine and Eve rushed into the room to where he was crouched.

Eve asked, "What is it?"

"I think it's a hidden door." Theron ran his fingers along the floor next to the piece of metal. He could feel a groove at the bottom, and air brushing across his skin. There was definitely an opening.

Caine was searching along the wall for the rest of the door outline. "I can't feel a split in the wood."

Theron stood, examining the wall and the groove he had discovered. "Get out of the way."

Caine jumped back just as Theron put his foot through the wood, making a big hole.

"That works," Eve said, backing up so Theron and Caine could yank the rest of the wood away around the hole, making it big enough for them to walk through.

Done, Theron peered into the black hole. Clapping his hands together, he formed a ball of witch light and pushed his hands into the dark.

"There are stairs leading down."

Anticipation fueled the pounding of his heart. He was close to finding Lyra. He could feel it. Goose bumps crawled over his skin and he shivered.

Caine spoke into his radio. "We found a secret set of stairs leading into a basement in the east wing, far hallway, collection room. Everyone reassemble here ASAP."

Theron stepped through the wall onto the first stone stair.

"Theron, wait. We'll all go together."

"I can't wait. Lyra is down there, hurt or worse."

"And what if the mistress is down there?" Caine asked.

"Then I'll kill her." Without waiting for a response, he continued down the steps, his hand out, lighting the way.

The stairs curved down into a dark and dank stone cavern. The smell of damp earth and old blood floated to him on a cool puff of musty air. Using the witch light, he looked around the room. It reminded him of a dungeon from the old days, carved out of rock, complete with iron manacles on the wall and a stone altar right in the middle.

Forcing down the bile rising in his throat, Theron neared the altar. It was stained dark red with blood. But when he got closer he realized to his relief that the stain was old, not fresh.

The others pounded down the steps as he crossed the cavernous room to a corridor leading farther into the rock.

"Lyra?" he called, as he moved down the dark passage. His voice echoed back to him.

He stopped at a closed wooden door. His heart pounding and his throat dry, he kicked it open, expecting to discover the worst. Splinters flew from the broken wood. He rushed inside to see an empty cot and more dark stains on the floor. Turning, he rushed out of the room and to the next closed door. He kicked that one in. Empty. Then the next and the next. All four cells were empty.

The passage ended. There was no other way out.

Backtracking, Theron walked back to the main stone room. The whole team had assembled around the altar. Caine was scraping the old blood into an evidence bag.

They turned and looked at Theron when he entered.

"We'll find her," Caine said. He glanced at Jace. "Was she ever here, Jace?"

Lifting his nose, Jace inhaled deeply, let it out, then did it again. He shook his head. "I don't get her scent down here at all."

"Okay, we'll continue searching the rest of the house."

They only had six hours left. The clock was ticking.

Lyra didn't know how long she lay on her back on the cement floor bleeding, but it was enough time to form a pool of blood the size of an orange around her head.

The wound on her neck throbbed, aching in time with the beat of her heart. She'd been bitten; blood sucked out of her, and now she lay virtually immobile while more blood dribbled from the open gouge on her throat.

Lifting her hand, she covered the wound, hoping to salvage some magical energy to heal it. She gathered the power inside her, but found it impossible to harness for her purposes. Something was blocking her. The wards on the room were slowly leaking over her. That was why she couldn't contact her gran and why now, she couldn't heal herself. She couldn't do magic at all.

She was powerless to do anything but await her fate.

Curling onto her side, she pulled her knees to her chest and wrapped her arms around them. She rocked against the despair overwhelming her.

Theron had to be looking for her. She knew he would scour the city to find her. She felt it in her heart and in her soul. But she also felt the time ticking away, like drops of water from a leaky tap. Soon it would stop. And she'd be dead.

The door to her prison creaked open again.

"It's time, witch, to die."

Chapter 31

After another three hours of searching the mistress's house, they had found nothing. No other secret rooms or stone altars. Nothing. A call to Monty revealed the same outcome from the search at Nadja's.

Now they were driving back to the lab to pursue a new path. Theron was desperately aware that they were running out of time. The sun had set and the moon was glowing like a beacon in the night. Except this beacon wasn't leading them to Lyra.

He rode in the back of the SUV with Eve and stared out the window as Caine maneuvered the downtown streets. Mahina drove in another vehicle behind them. Large buildings and neon signs flashed by him without notice. How could he concentrate on anything when Lyra was out there somewhere waiting for him to rescue her?

Sucking in a breath, he tried to stop the images of her battered body lying on a cement slab—her sightless eyes looking at him in accusation. *You did this to me!* They screamed at him. He covered his face in his hands to rub the thoughts out of his mind. He had to stifle a despairing cry.

"Theron, pull it together," Caine demanded. "You can't help Lyra if you can't function."

He dropped his hands to his lap and clenched his jaw. He was losing it. Helplessness threatened to consume him. He'd never experienced pain as severe before.

Eve grabbed his hand. "It's going to be okay. Lyra is strong. She won't go down without a fight."

"How did you escape?"

Startled by the question, she looked at Caine then down at her lap. "Caine found me."

"Did you know he would come for you?"

She nodded. "Yes."

"How did you know?"

"Because I knew he loved me and wouldn't stop until he found me. That's what kept me going."

"And if you hadn't known that he loved you, would you have fought so hard to stay alive?"

Tears rolled down her cheeks, as she squeezed his hand. "She knows you love her, Theron."

"I never got the chance to tell her." His voice hitched in his throat. Embarrassed, he returned his gaze to the window.

"It doesn't matter. A woman knows when her man loves her. She knows."

Nodding, Theron couldn't look back at Eve. He stared at the moon and prayed that Lyra knew how he felt. Prayed she would fight until he came to get her.

As they zipped down another street and turned a corner, something made Theron turn to look out of the window. The same voice from the other night whispered in his ear.

Look and see.

One of the tall buildings caught Theron's eye. He'd seen that exact sign somewhere else.

"Stop!"

"What?" Caine called.

"Stop! Stop. Pull over to the curb."

Lurching to the side, Caine applied the brakes and parked by the curb. Theron opened his door and jumped out onto the sidewalk. He ran down the street a block and looked up at the billboard on the side of the skyscraper. He had flashes of the same sign in his head.

Caine, Eve and Mahina came alongside him and they all looked at the sign. Caine asked, "What's going on?"

"I recognize that sign."

"From where?"

"I think from when I touched Lori James. I think it's one of her memories."

Caine spun around and frowned. Eve did the same and asked, "Hey, aren't we close to Shadowwood?"

"It's down two blocks," he said, then perked up and grabbed Theron's arm. "I don't know why I didn't think of it before. Nadja owns the studio. Come on!"

They ran back to the SUV. Caine pulled a U-turn in front of thick traffic and took the next corner at high speed. Within moments, he drove onto the curb and parked in front of a nondescript brick building with a small sign. *Shadowwood Studios.*

On the way, Mahina had radioed Jace and Tala in the other SUV and told them to meet at the studio. As Theron jumped out of the vehicle, Jace screeched to a stop on the curb behind them.

Now, the six of them assembled outside the main door to the studio. Mahina and Tala checked the clips on their guns.

Theron followed Jace and Tala down the alleyway and around to the back entrance of the music studio. His whole body shook with restrained fury.

Jace kicked open the door, then Tala went in, gun pointed. Jace followed her through, Theron at his back.

Murmuring under his breath, Theron rubbed his hands together hard. After a few moments, smoke began to rise from them.

One of the lycan security guards, who had advanced on them from a side room, noticed his movements. "What are you doing?"

Theron continued to invoke the spell, rubbing his hands harder and faster.

The guards glanced at one another nervously, then looked down at their gun hands. Smoke rose from their flesh. They both released their weapons, snatching their hands to their chests. Even from where Theron stood he could see the angry red burns on the guards' hands.

Capitalizing on the opportunity Theron had given them, Tala and Jace subdued both the guards with well-aimed punches to the head.

Once the lycans were down, Tala, Jace and Theron proceeded into the main studio area. Caine had another guard dangling by his neck. The guard's face was quickly turning purple as the vampire crushed his throat. After two more seconds, the lycan was unconscious and Caine let him fall to the ground.

"It's all clear in the back," Tala said.

Loud, pulse-pounding music resonated. The musicians were obviously oblivious to what was happening outside the main recording studio.

Theron yanked the door to the studio open, where four young men were playing, and walked in.

Startled, one of the guitarists stopped his riff and stared at him. "Who the hell are you, dude?"

With the guitar riff absent, the rest of the band finally noticed the intrusion.

"Where's the door to the basement?" Theron commanded.

"Whoa, man, you can't come in here," the singer said, walking toward Theron, his hand clenched into a fist.

Caine stepped into the studio beside Theron. The singer stopped, his face growing even paler than it was. "Well, if it isn't the boys from Crimson Strain."

"We haven't done anything, man," the drummer whined.

"Where's Nadja?"

"I don't know." The singer shrugged. "She said we could hang here and practice as long as wanted."

Caine frowned then nodded. "As the man said, get out."

Without another word, the four band members set down their instruments and rushed out of the studio.

Once they were gone, Theron pushed aside the keyboards and drum set, surveying the floor. Panic took hold of him. Glancing at the clock on the wall, he saw that it was eleven o'clock. They only had an hour before Lyra would be sacrificed. This was their last chance to find her. Dropping to all fours, he scoured the floor, feeling his way with this hands.

"Theron?" He heard the inflection in Caine's voice. The sympathy. He didn't want it. He wasn't going to give up.

"She's here. I can feel her." He glanced at them, tears started to well in his eyes. His heart squeezed. His gut churned. Deep, slicing pain slashed through him to his soul. He would wither away and die if he didn't find Lyra. Without her, he was nothing. "She's here. I know it."

Caine, Eve and Tala dropped to their knees to help him search the floor. Jace and Mahina started looking along the walls.

Time ticked by as they searched the room. It sounded like metal clanging in Theron's ears. Madness closed in on him. He could sense it knocking on his mind. His hands shook, and sweat dripped off his face onto the floor. He couldn't concentrate. He was becoming manic.

Jumping to his feet, he rushed the far wall and tore at the multitude of band and concert posters plastered on the wall. He ripped and tore, shredding whatever he could get his fingers on. Maybe if he tore enough away his heart wouldn't hurt, the agony of Lyra's loss wouldn't eat away at him, little by little.

He ripped another of Nadja's posters down, his fingertips brushing against a rut. He stopped and stared at the wall. There was a separation in the wood, and it went all the way to the floor.

"I found it!" he called, tearing away the rest of the paper to reveal a door.

There was no handle, so as a team they pried it open with their fingers. A yellow glow radiated up from the stairs. Theron couldn't hold on any longer. He rushed down the steps, dread crawling over his skin.

When he got to the bottom, his breath whooshed out of his lungs and he thought he'd been pushed over the edge into madness.

Twelve cloaked figures were standing in a semi-circle. Lyra was there—naked and bound to a stone altar they surrounded. And lording over her, with skin as black and oily as tar and fangs dripping with saliva, was the creature from his nightmares.

It smiled at him—as if welcoming the company.

Chapter 32

Lethargic but determined, Lyra pulled on the leather bindings strapping her to the unyielding stone slab just as Theron rushed into the room. Tears rolled down her cheeks at the sight of him. She knew he'd come for her.

"Welcome, Theron LeNoir," Lady Ankara Jannali hissed above Lyra, her voice no longer distinguished as female. "You're just in time to witness the birth of a new era."

Theron raised his hands. Lyra saw the telltale red glow of magic around his fingertips. Except she didn't think the spell worked, because the creature above her started to laugh.

Theron's face fell and he started to back away. His hands went to his throat.

"You cannot best me with your mediocre magical ability. Your father told me all about your skills, boy, but you are no match for me. I have been casting spells for thousands of years."

Lyra cried out as she watched Theron struggle against a phantom hand squeezing his neck. He clawed at the air, his face quickly turning purple.

Her vision faded in and out as she continued to pull on her restraints. Blood loss had made her weak. She could barely lift her head, but she had to fight to stay alive. She had to give Theron a reason to hold on.

Shots rang out, echoing in the lofty room as the rest of the OCU burst in. Tala, Mahina and Eve at the head, guns pointed. The mistress stumbled back as three silver bullets penetrated her body. One hit her in the shoulder, the other two in her chest. None of them seemed to do much damage; she was still on her feet, growling like a rabid animal.

Lyra searched the room for Theron. He was slumped against the far wall, but alive. She could see the slow rise and fall of his chest. Perhaps the bullets were enough of a distraction to stop Ankara from killing Theron.

They were certainly enough to prompt the rest of the contingent into action. Within seconds there was a full-out battle raging in the room. Jace, Tala and Mahina all shifted into wolves and launched at the cloaked figures. Lyra could hear the grunts, groans and yelps of pain all around her as the fight ensued.

If she could manage to free a hand, she might be able to help the others. At least she could rescue herself. She yanked on the leather strap, twisting and turning her wrist to loosen the knot. The leather cut into her skin. Blood dotted the stone beneath her arm. Pain ripped through her. But she continued on. She needed to get free. Theron needed her.

After a few more turns, the loop around her hand loosened. Setting her arm down, she folded her thumb over her palm and pulled her hand free. Glorying in her achievement, she worked at the tie on her other wrist. She pulled and yanked and twisted, but couldn't get it free. She'd have to try the same technique.

Desperation filled her heart and she turned to find Theron. He still lay against the wall and hadn't moved.

She reached toward him, stretching as far as she could. "Theron," she screamed.

He remained motionless.

Tears rolled freely as she closed her eyes and searched her soul for the magic she would need. Curling it into a ball, she harnessed the energy and tried to move it down her arm to her fingertips.

Opening her eyes, she stretched her arm out again toward Theron. Pulling on her other arm, she cried out at the sickening pop of her shoulder joint. But despite the pain tearing through her, she reached out to him and threw the ball of magic.

She watched as it hit him in the chest and spread over his whole form, like a rapidly spreading energy blanket. She prayed it would work.

"Theron! Wake up!"

His eyes snapped open.

Her heart leapt in her throat and she began to smile, but a hand clamping down over her mouth cut it off.

"Going somewhere, witch?"

Lyra struggled against the force holding her down, but the mistress was too strong. She leered down at Lyra, her cruel black lips split into a blood-freezing grin.

"It's almost midnight. I don't want you missing all the fun, since *you* are the main attraction."

Lyra fought against the hold on her, thrashing her legs and arms. She raked her nails across the mistress's arm with her free hand. It had no effect.

Still grinning, Ankara raised her arm over Lyra. In her hand, she held a long silver ceremonial dagger. A horned beast carved into the glinted blade.

Shaking her head, Lyra watched in horror as the knife came down. This was it. She was going to die. There was no stopping it. She hadn't fought hard enough. Theron hadn't come soon enough. Now she was going to die without being able to tell him how much she loved him. How much she wanted to start a life with him.

Squeezing her eyes shut, Lyra prepared for the pain to come. She took in a deep breath as the blade plunged into her stomach.

But the pain never came.

Opening her eyes, Lyra looked down at her belly in disbelief. The razor-sharp dagger point hovered one inch from the soft flesh of her stomach. The mistress couldn't bring it down any farther.

Theron had formed a protection bubble over her.

Shrieking, the mistress reared back, removing her hand from Lyra's mouth, and lifted the knife high over her head to bring it back down, this time aiming at her throat. The bubble couldn't sustain the level of force and power Lyra knew the mistress possessed.

Terror-filled, Lyra sucked in a breath as the blade came down. Theron appeared in front of her, shielding her from the killing blow. She grasped his hand and, in the blink of an eye, fed more magic into him than she'd ever produced. A blaze roared inside her. Searing agony ripped through her inside and out as energy flowed from her into Theron.

Together.

Theron's and her gran's voices melded as one in her mind.

Together you can make it right. Together you are strong. Together your magic can go from dark to light, make things right from wrong.

Time stood still as the blade came down. She could see every inch it descended, closer and closer to Theron's back. He wouldn't survive the wound if it pierced the magical shield and slid into him. No amount of healing magic could fix an injury so grave.

She squeezed his hand and stared into his eyes. She saw in them what she'd been looking for her whole life—unconditional love and understanding. She saw her soul reflected back in the swirling gray depths of his eyes. And she lost herself completely to him. In that moment, they became one.

The dagger never found its mark. In a blaze of blue light, the mistress was thrown back, the knife melted in her hand. Screeching, she scratched at her eyes while they seemed to dissolve from her face.

With a bloodcurdling scream, she fell to the floor, sliding in and out of her true form. Half her body formed the black-skinned demon and the other the radiant vampire beauty. As she cowered on the ground, clawing at her deformed body, Caine and the others crowded around her.

"Is she dead?" Lyra asked, her body shaking uncontrollably.

Smoothing her hair from her forehead, Theron glanced over his shoulder. "Not yet. But she will be before long."

Caine turned and looked at Lyra. "We'll take care of it, Lyra." He gestured to Theron. "Get her out of here."

Without another word, Theron untied her and was

carrying her up the stairs. Tears rimmed his eyes as he murmured into her neck, *"Ma petite sorcière,* my love."

With a full heart, Lyra wrapped her arms around Theron and let him take her away to safety. As they moved through the cellar, she saw several other bodies on the floor—the coconspirators in Ankara's bid to open the gates of hell and release her fellow demons. Nadja Devanshi lay unmoving, her eyes wide and her throat ripped out. She wondered who had had the pleasure of that kill. She also recognized Nadja's lawyer. Mortally wounded, he met her gaze, but she turned away, not giving him the attention he wanted. He didn't deserve her pity. None of them did. They had reaped what they had sowed.

Once up the stairs and out of the studio, they were greeted by several police cruisers and a couple of ambulances.

Laal rushed over to them, his hands fluttering like a butterfly. "Let's get a medic here," he yelled.

Two paramedics ran their way. But Lyra didn't want them to touch her. She was safe in Theron's arms and that was all that mattered.

"Put her over here," one of them said.

Lyra shook her head and gripped Theron tighter. "No, don't let them take me. I don't want to go to the hospital. I want to go home with you."

"Shh, it's okay, Lyra. You're safe." He set her down on the stretcher.

"Don't let me go." She grasped his hand tight.

He pressed his lips to the tip of her nose. "I won't. Ever."

That was the last thing she heard him say before a wave of nausea swept over her and pulled her down into oblivion.

Chapter 33

The warm afternoon breeze rustled the strands of hair around Lyra's face as she pulled the weeds surrounding her tomato plants. She raised her face to the wind and inhaled deeply. It felt heavenly to be outside in her garden after being cooped up inside for the past two days healing.

Her wrist, which she had badly sprained, still pained her if she exerted herself too much, but the skin on her arms and hands that had been burned by the flow of magic had fully healed. Thanks to Theron's special healing ointment. If only he were here to revel in his labors. Unfortunately, she hadn't heard from him in three days. The last time she saw him was when he handed her off to the paramedic.

She stabbed her rake in the dirt and yanked another weed out. That was how she felt right now. Raked and stabbed and yanked on. Her heart couldn't handle much more.

Three days ago, she had awakened in her bedroom. Caine, Eve, Jace and Tala had been there, standing around her bed waiting for her to wake up. She'd learned that Theron had set her up at home with her own doctor and nurse, instead of going to the hospital, just as she had asked. But he had been absent.

Caine told her Theron had returned home, but assured her he'd be back. She wanted to believe it, but ninety-six hours later she was having her doubts.

Trust your heart, Lyra.

"My heart's not doing too well right now, Gran. So you'll excuse me if I don't fully trust."

You of all people should know that what you see with your eyes isn't always true.

Lyra stood and brushed at the dirt clinging to her cotton pants. "Please don't philosophize with me today. I'm really not in the mood for cryptic nonsense." She moved to the next row of vegetables, knelt down in the soil and started to dig out the unwanted plants.

He loves you, darling. Have faith in that.

Sighing, Lyra wiped at the hair tickling her nose with the back of her gloved hand. "Sometimes that's not enough to believe in."

She took in another whiff of perfumed air and tried not to notice the pain in her chest. She had no idea that heartache actually hurt in the chest cavity. Every time she breathed or moved she wanted to cry. As if there were a string attached to her tear ducts from her heart. She hated the feeling. But couldn't stop it. There was no spell or charm to make the agony disappear. Being in love was a whole different sort of pain.

A throb at her wrist gave her pause and she stopped her work. Stripping off her canvas gloves, Lyra rubbed at her injury. The effort of yanking on her restraints had done a number on her wrist.

As she stroked her tender skin, she gloried in the fact that they had won. The bad guys had been caught and justice would be served. The mistress had died of her injuries. And Lyra thanked the Goddess for it. The thought of that demon being alive and able to manipulate and maneuver even behind jailhouse bars literally made her sick.

Councilmen of Necropolis were already looking for a new mayor. Lyra shook her head, knowing that Laal had already tossed his hat in the ring. Funny thing was, she'd probably vote for him. He had come through for the OCU in the end, and she realized that he really did have the lab's best interests at heart. And it wasn't as if he would be worse than the mistress. At least they all knew that Laal was definitely a vampire and not something foreign or malevolent, like a demon.

He was a pompous ass, but at least he wouldn't murder people to open a gateway to hell.

Everything was getting back to normal after almost a year of turbulence in the lab, and murder and mayhem on the streets. The main lab was being rebuilt. Gwen was up and around, already complaining about the job the construction workers were doing with her space. Rick, her human devotee, was running after her, doting on her like a lovesick puppy.

Jace and Tala had even been by earlier to tell her that they were expecting a baby. And that they wanted Lyra to be the spiritual guardian. She'd been touched and ended up sobbing into Tala's shoulder. Tala had just patted Lyra's back, likely suspecting that her tears were from more than just their pregnancy. Once they left—Jace in a hurry after Lyra's display—Lyra wiped her eyes dry and promised herself she wouldn't cry again…at least for the rest of the day.

But when she stood up, brushed again at her pants and turned toward the patio deck, she suspected she wasn't going to be able to keep that promise.

"*Bonjour,* Lyra."

She nearly sighed at the sight of him. In khaki pants and a dark green polo shirt, his hair unbound and rustling in the breeze, he looked damn sexy standing on her deck with a box of small plants in his arms. Heart racing, she walked toward him, wiping at the dirt she was certain was streaked all over her face.

"I brought you some herbs that I knew you didn't have." He set the box on top of the picnic table. "I brought some wormwood, motherwort, hawthorn and a few others from my own garden. A talented witch should have these things."

He rubbed his hands on his pants nervously as she moved to stand in front of him. She took in everything about him, afraid that he would disappear, as if he were an illusion conjured up from her unconscious mind.

He met her gaze and she could see the nerves zinging through the stormy gray depths. "You look better. How are you feeling?"

She showed him her hands and arms. "Almost healed."

"*Bon.*" He rubbed a hand over his mouth. "I heard everyone received their just rewards."

She nodded. "Ankara is dead. Nadja, too. Everyone else is stewing in a jail cell."

"The captain found the bomber, *oui?*"

"Yeah. It ended up being one of Gwen's assistants. A vampiress heavily under Nadja's influence. She'd only been working with us for eight months."

"I'm sorry to hear that."

"Gwen's taking it the hardest. She thought she should've known of the girl's intentions."

He nodded. "Yes, well, we cannot always know people's intentions."

"No, we can't." Lyra struggled not to cry. All she wanted to do was wrap herself in the warmth and security of Theron's arms. But at this point she couldn't really be sure of that security.

He must've heard the inflection in her voice because he put his hand up to stop her from saying anything further. "Let me talk before you yell at me, slap me or walk away from me. Or maybe you want to do all three."

"Theron—"

"Please, Lyra, let me finish."

"Okay." She sat at the picnic table, realizing that her knees were wobbling and wouldn't support her for long anyway.

"D'accord." He started to pace in front of her, wringing his fingers together. "First, I apologize for leaving suddenly without a word, but you were unconscious and I had to return home to see about my father. After what the mistress inferred about him, I had to make sure he wasn't involved with any of this."

"And was he?"

"No. He may be an immoral, reprehensible man, but he's not psychotic with delusions of godhood." He ran a hand through his hair. "Secondly, I was scared of my feelings for you, so I needed some distance to reconcile them, figure them out, put them into perspective."

"And are they reconciled?"

"*Oui,* very much so." He stopped pacing and stood, gazing down at her intently. Nerves suddenly gripped her and she started to quiver. "And lastly, I had to return home for this."

He held out his hand, palm up. Craning her neck, she looked into it. There was nothing there. Keeping her gaze, he waved his other hand over his palm, and when she looked again, a small circular piece of silver sat in his hand.

It was a ring. The most beautiful ring she'd ever seen in her entire life. It was the ring from Theron's collection. The one she'd wished a man would give to her one day. This man.

Tears brimming in her eyes, she reached for it, but it disappeared before she could touch it.

"Where did it go?" she asked, panic grasping her tight.

Kneeling down, Theron took her left hand and held it in his. "Right where it should be."

She looked down at her hand and saw the ring on her finger. It warmed her skin where it touched.

"*Mon couer entier.* My whole heart and more. I've never wanted anything in my whole life as much as I want you, *ma petite sorcière.* Will you do the honor of being my wife?"

She nodded, unable to form words. "You had me at 'I brought you some herbs.'"

Grinning, Theron stood and wrapped her in his arms, pressing her so close she could hear the thumping of his heart. A sound she gloried in hearing again. It sounded pure and perfect, and she vowed never to mistrust it again.

Cupping her cheeks with his hands, he said, "I am

completely and utterly in love with you, Lyra Magice. Everything about you is magical."

Sighing, she fisted her hands in his hair and brought his mouth to hers. She kissed him with everything she had, and everything she was. Here was her soul mate, and she finally felt complete.

Destiny, darling. Destiny.

They both pulled away and Theron said, "Eleanore is a very wise woman."

Wide-eyed, Lyra stared at Theron. "You can hear her?"

"Yes." Smiling, Theron swept her up into his arms and carried her across the deck to the balcony doors. "But I'm hoping she'll give us some privacy, for let's say, four hours. There are many things I need to show you."

"Like what?"

Nuzzling her ear, he whispered into it.

The blush rose from the tips of her toes to the top of her head. "Are you sure that's even possible?" she stuttered, sweat already starting to trickle down her back at the prospect of what he proposed.

He nibbled on her chin. "Trust me. We'll figure it out."

She did trust him. Mind, body and soul.

Sliding open the glass door with his foot, Theron carried her across the threshold and into the house.

* * * * *

Be sure to watch for Vivi Anna's
next scintillating romance,
ICE BOUND,
which will be part of the
WINTER KISSED *anthology,*
coming only to Silhouette Nocturne
in November '08.
And now for a sneak preview of
ICE BOUND,
please turn the page.

At first, big fat flakes floated down, carefree and lazy, but Dr. Darien Calder knew that was just the preshow. The dark sky threatened so much more than the pretty flakes of storybook Christmases. After the first fall, the wind picked up and started to howl. At one point it became so fierce, Darien had trouble keeping the SUV on the road.

As visibility dropped close to zero, Darien slowed the vehicle down to ten miles an hour. He prayed silently that there was no one else stupid enough to be out on the roads. Even at this speed, a head-on collision would definitely cause some injuries.

A brutal gust of wind howled against the glass, rattling the vehicle. Darien could feel the cold creeping over his body. Even through his hat, gloves and heavy thermal jacket, the cold seeped in. He went to turn up the dial on the heater, but stopped when he realized it was already cranked to the maximum.

He'd been to the coldest places on earth—Antarctica, the North Pole, Greenland—but for some reason it felt colder here in Kushiro. Maybe that was because he couldn't get the sense of trepidation out of his system. Something was going to happen.

He shook his head to clear it. "Don't be stupid, man. It's just a silly story."

Even though he said the words, he didn't fully feel the conviction behind them.

He had come to Japan to study the environment and to learn more about the legend that had haunted him, had invaded his dreams nightly, from the moment he learned of it—the legend of Koori-Ona. It told of a beautiful, ghostly woman appearing to lost travelers in snowstorms, who with one kiss from her icy lips, literally froze the doomed from the inside out.

Ever since he had heard about the ice-maiden myth, he'd done some research on it. Like everything he did, he approached it with a clinical mind. But there was no sound reasoning behind the myth. It was a story and nothing more. Even *if* she visited him in his dreams.

He'd gone on too long without a woman—that was all. He was just lonely. He was pathetic if just the mention of a beautiful woman incited hot dreams. And they'd been extremely hot. He'd woken up a few times, harder than steel.

"Like a damn teenager." He chuckled to himself. He really was pathetic.

No wonder Jessica had left him all those months ago. She accused him of being too wrapped up in his work, and she'd been right. If he wasn't out in the field doing studies, he was at home in his office writing about his studies on his laptop, or he had his nose in a research book preparing for his next time out in the field.

He'd gone too long without a healthy relationship. Maybe when he got to Tokyo, he'd go to one of those gentlemen's clubs and acquire some female companionship for the night. Something uncomplicated and temporary. Just enough company to break him out of his dry spell.

As he mused over the possibilities, bright lights flashed at him through the windshield. Another vehicle was bearing down on him and at high speed.

Cursing, Darien wrenched on the steering wheel. There was no traction on the road. It was pure ice.

He tried to correct the spin he put the vehicle in, but it was too late. He plowed into a huge snowdrift on the side of the road before he could even think.

From the impact, he knocked his head on the steering wheel. Thankfully, the air bag didn't pop. He didn't really want to deal with trying to shove it back into the wheel.

The SUV was still running. Darien put it in Reverse, but it didn't budge. The sound coming from the rear indicated that the tires were spinning in place. There was too much ice.

Cursing again, he banged his fist on the steering wheel, and then shifted it into Park. He was going to have to get out and put something behind the tires to give them some traction.

Pulling his hat down over his ears, Darien opened the door and jumped out of the SUV into the blizzard. As he made his way around to the back, he searched the surroundings for the other vehicle. There was no way that it hadn't also gone off the road. Not in this weather, not on this icy stretch of highway. But he couldn't see anything through the howling, blistering white wall of snow.

Opening the hatch on the SUV, he dug through the equipment and found a short-handled shovel, specially designed to dig out of snow and ice. He slammed the hatch shut and proceeded to dig the back tires out of the snow they were entrenched in.

After fifteen minutes of digging, Darien climbed back into the SUV and tried to back out. But it was no use. He was good and stuck.

Darien jumped out into the snow again to go around the back to the hatch. He'd grab some supplies to hunker down for a few hours. As he opened the back, a sound whispered to him on the wind. Shivers, not just from the cold, raced down his spine.

He turned to survey the area. Was there someone there calling to him? Maybe the driver of the other vehicle.

"Darien." The haunting voice echoed all around him. He stared into the blustering snow. Desperate to see something, anything, concrete.

Something caught his eye, and he turned toward it. A shape materialized in the blinding white.

"Darien, I've been waiting for you."

* * * * *

Here's a sneak peek at
THE CEO'S CHRISTMAS PROPOSITION,
the first in **USA TODAY** *bestselling author*
Merline Lovelace's **HOLIDAYS ABROAD** *trilogy,*
coming in November 2008.

American Devon McShay is about to get the
Christmas surprise of a lifetime when she meets
her new client, sexy billionaire Caleb Logan,
for the very first time.

Silhouette®

Desire

Available November 2008

Her breath whistled out in a sigh of relief when he exited Customs. Devon recognized him right away from the newspaper and magazine articles her friend and partner Sabrina had looked up during her frantic prep work.

Caleb John Logan, Jr. Thirty-one. Six-two. With jet-black hair, laser-blue eyes and a linebacker's shoulders under his charcoal-gray cashmere overcoat. His jaw-dropping good looks didn't score him any points with Devon. She'd learned the hard way not to trust hand-some heartbreakers like Cal Logan.

But he was a client. An important one. And she was willing to give someone who'd served a hitch in the marines before earning a B.S. from the University of Oregon, an MBA from Stanford and his first million at the ripe old age of twenty-six the benefit of the doubt.

Right up until he spotted the hot-pink pashmina, that is.

Devon knew the flash of color was more visible than the sign she held up with his name on it. So she wasn't surprised when Logan picked her out of the crowd and cut in her direction. She'd just plastered on her best businesswoman smile when he whipped an arm around her waist. The next moment she was sprawled against his cashmere-covered chest.

"Hello, brown eyes."

Swooping down, he covered her mouth with his.

Sheer astonishment kept Devon rooted to the spot for a few seconds while her mind whirled chaotically. Her first thought was that her client had downed a few too many drinks during the long flight. Her second, that he'd mistaken the kind of escort and consulting services her company provided. Her third shoved everything else out of her head.

The man could kiss!

His mouth moved over hers with a skill that ignited sparks at a half-dozen flash points throughout her body. Devon hadn't experienced that kind of spontaneous combustion in a while. A *long* while.

The sparks were still popping when she pushed off his chest, only now they fueled a flush of anger.

"Do you always greet women you don't know with a lip-lock, Mr. Logan?"

A smile crinkled the skin at the corners of his eyes. "As a matter of fact, I don't. That was from Don."

"Huh?"

"He said he owed you one from New Year's Eve two years ago and made me promise to deliver it."

She stared up at him in total incomprehension. Logan hooked a brow and attempted to prompt a non-existent memory.

"He abandoned you at the Waldorf. Five minutes before midnight. To deliver twins."

"I don't have a clue who or what you're…"

Understanding burst like a water balloon.

"Wait a sec. Are you talking about Sabrina's old boyfriend? Your buddy, who's now an ob-gyn doc?"

It was Logan's turn to look startled. He recovered faster than Devon had, though. His smile widened into a rueful grin.

"I take it you're not Sabrina Russo."

"No, Mr. Logan, I am *not*."

* * * * *

Be sure to look for
THE CEO'S CHRISTMAS PROPOSITION
by Merline Lovelace
Available in November 2008
wherever books are sold,
including most bookstores, supermarkets,
drugstores and discount stores